TOBY GOES BANANAS

TOBY GOES BANANAS

by Franck Girard
& Serge Bloch

graphix
An Imprint of
SCHOLASTIC

Additional text by Adam Rau

Library of Congress Control Number: 2016957246

ISBN 978-0-545-85284-5 (hardcover)
ISBN 978-0-545-85283-8 (paperback)

10 9 8 7 6 5 4 3 2 1 17 18 19 20 21

Printed in China 38
First edition, July 2017
Edited by Adam Rau
Book design by Phil Falco
Creative Director: David Saylor

HI! My name is Toby.

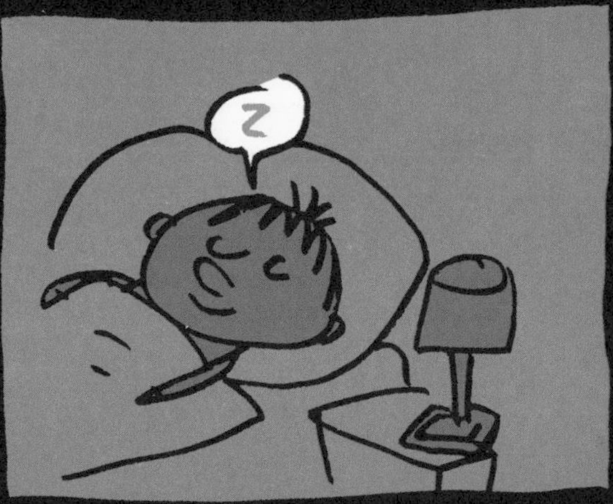

Z

That's me asleep.

I'm probably dreaming right now.
I'm not sure about what.

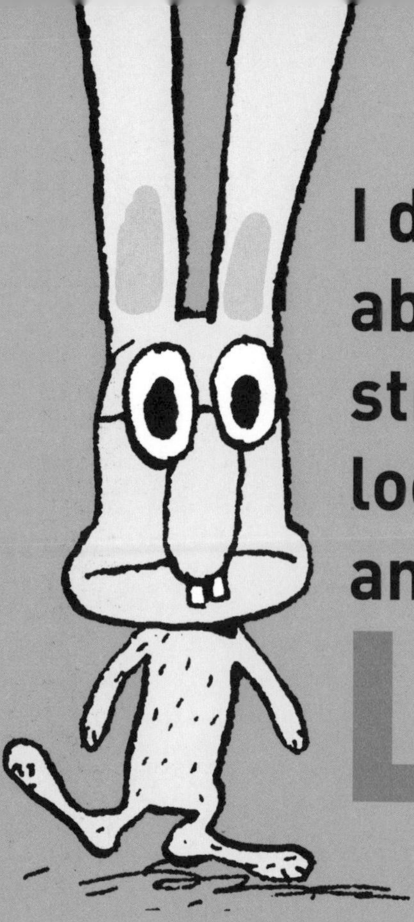

I dream about strange-looking animals a **LOT.**

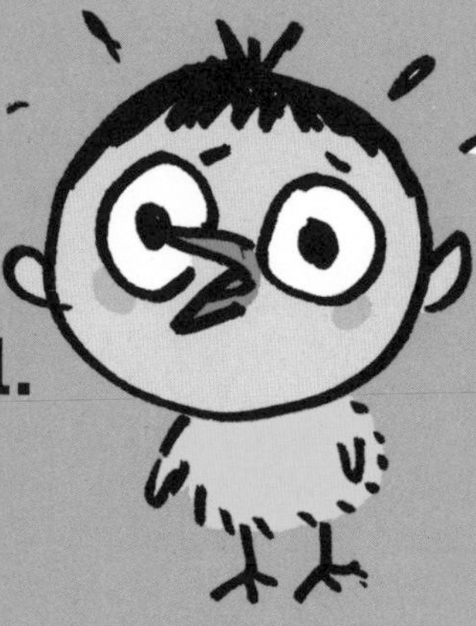

Or ME as an animal.

(Don't ask me why, because I have NO idea.)

This is the BEST part of the day.

No worries, no parents, no teachers, no quizzes. Just me, my pillow, and my weird dreams. I don't want anything from anyone and no one wants anything from me.

AHHHH. Pure bliss.

But it never lasts.

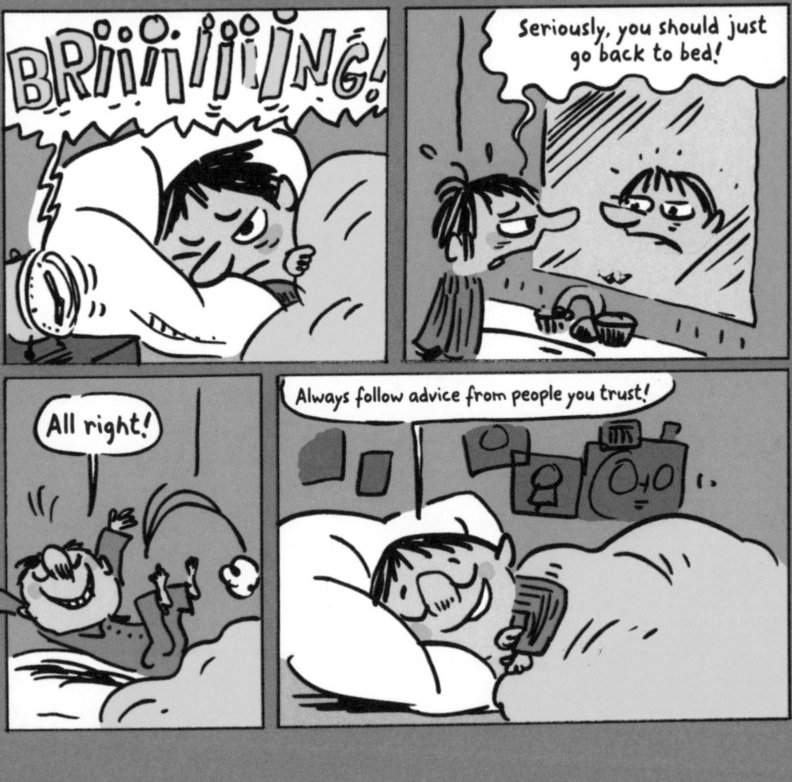
BRIIIIIIIIING!
Seriously, you should just go back to bed!
All right!
Always follow advice from people you trust!

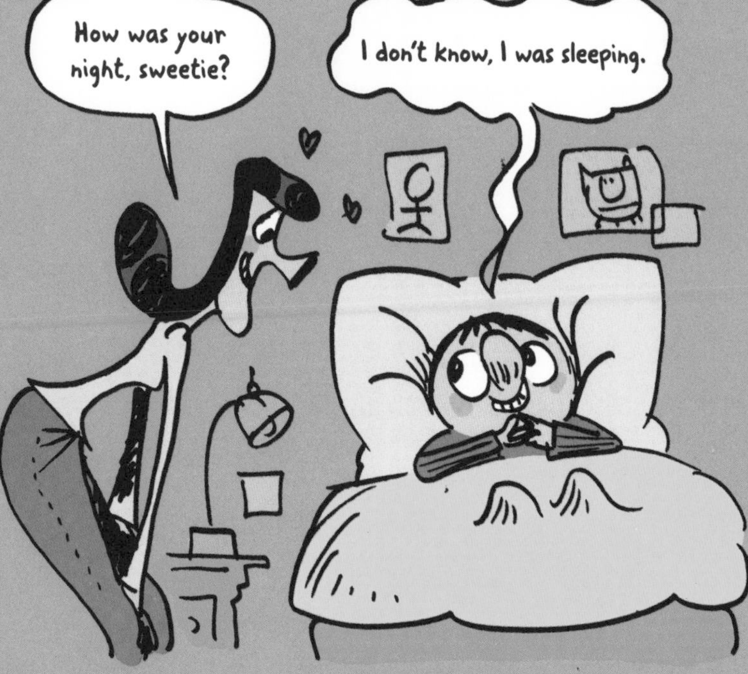
How was your night, sweetie?
I don't know, I was sleeping.

It's not always easy to get going in the morning. The last thing I want to do is go to school. Some kids love it. That's good for them.

I guess . . .

Mom always has breakfast ready,
which helps me wake up. And she's
a pretty good cook. I mean, she
makes the best bowl of cereal
I've EVER had!

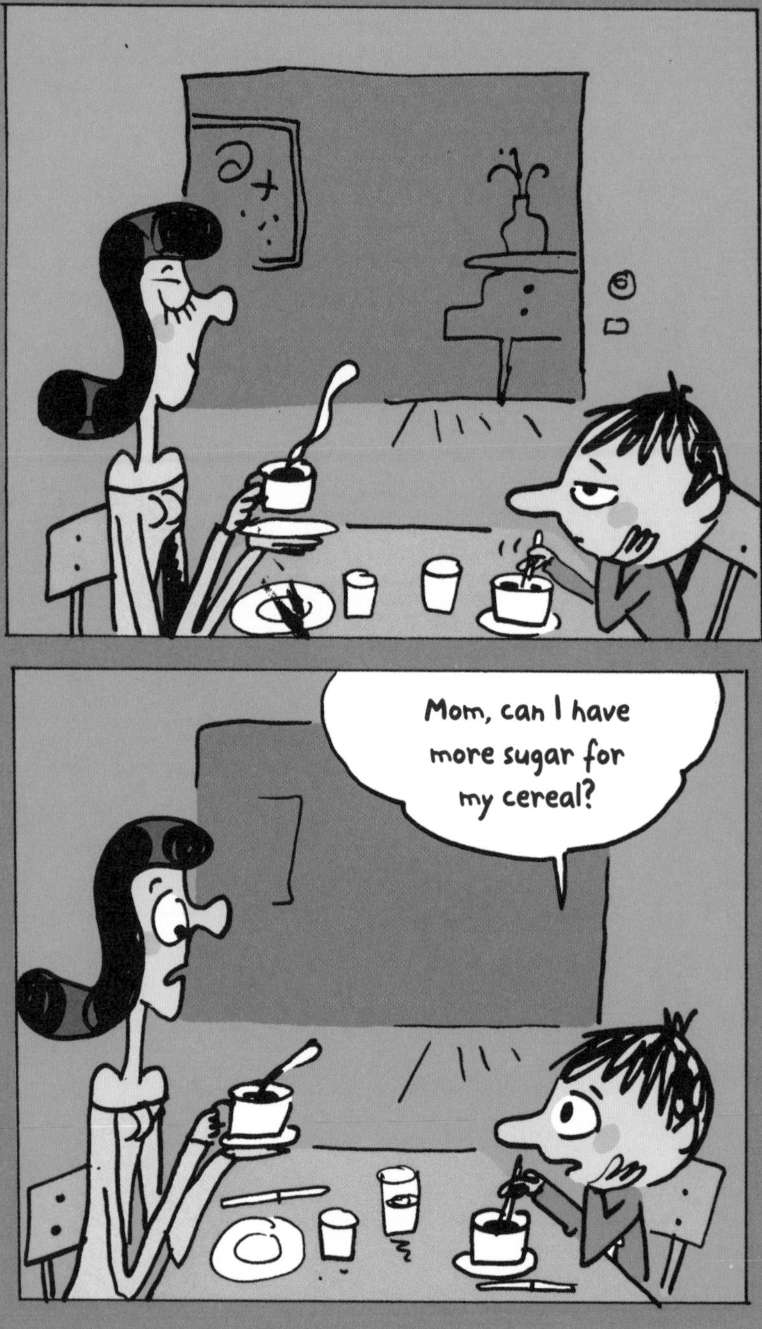
Mom, can I have more sugar for my cereal?

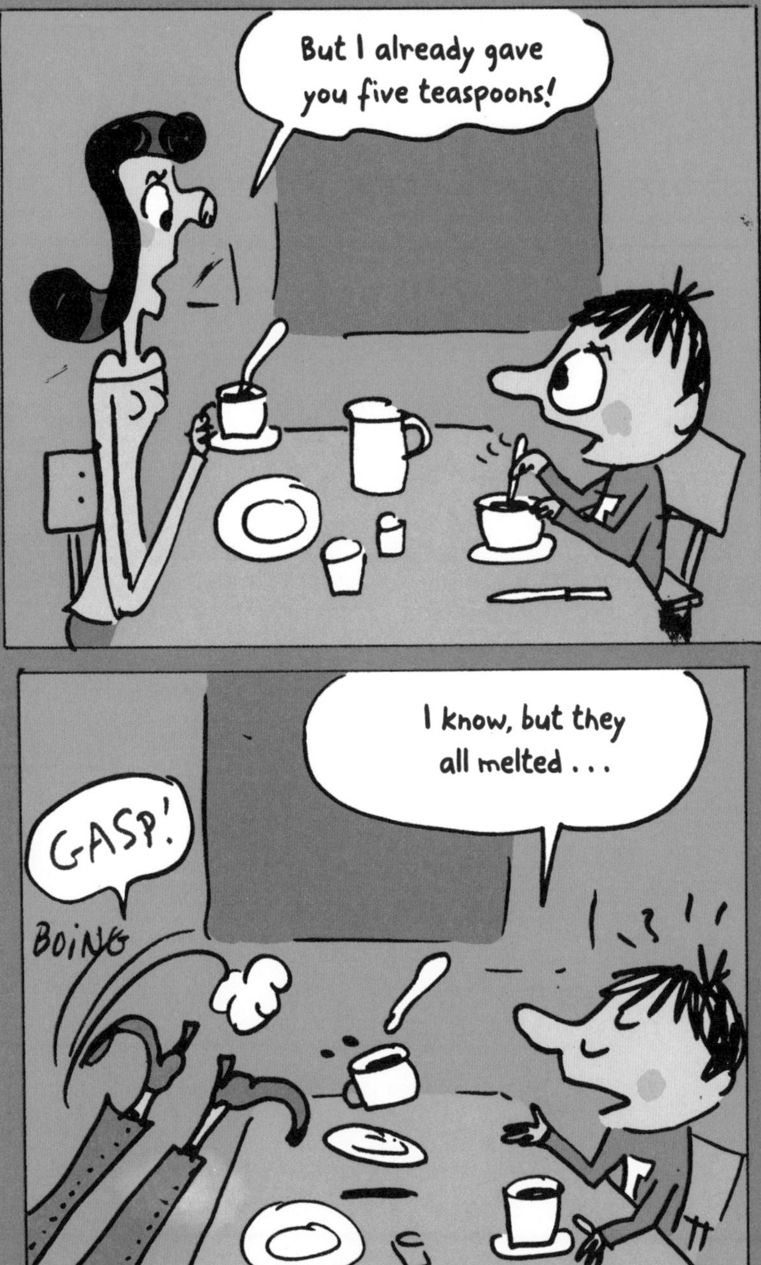
But I already gave you five teaspoons!
I know, but they all melted . . .
GASP!
BOING

I suppose this is as good a place as any to introduce my family. **They're pretty good people, as far as families go. No real stinkers in the bunch. You could say I got lucky.**

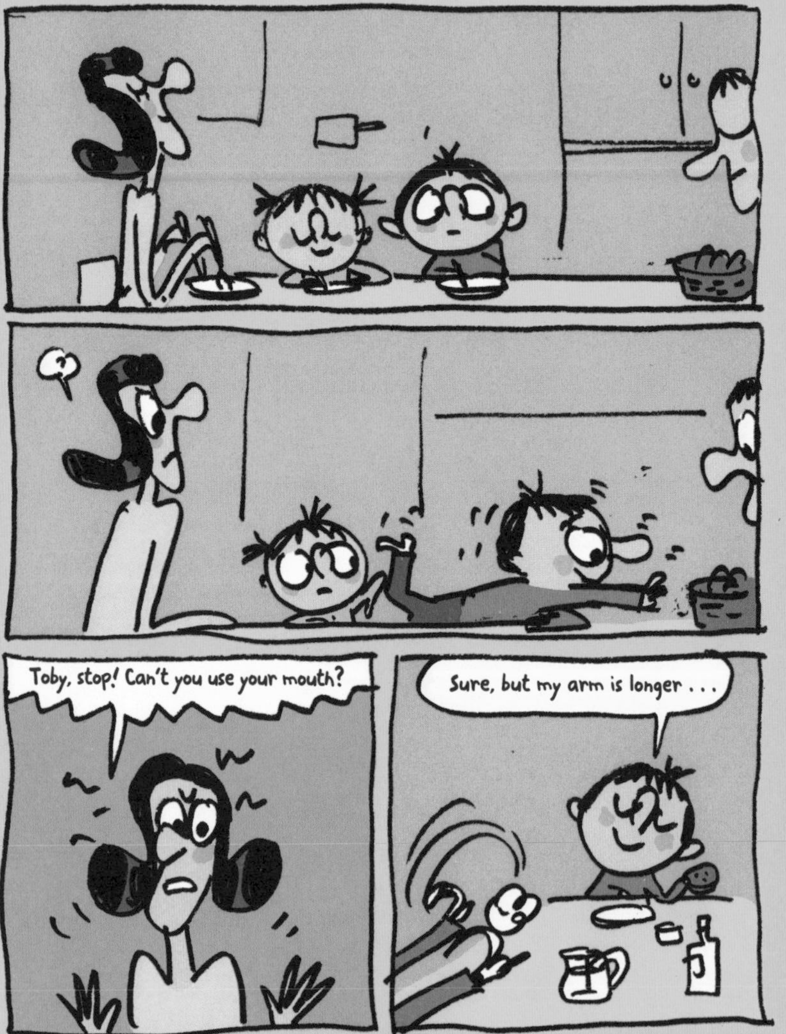

Toby, stop! Can't you use your mouth?
Sure, but my arm is longer . . .

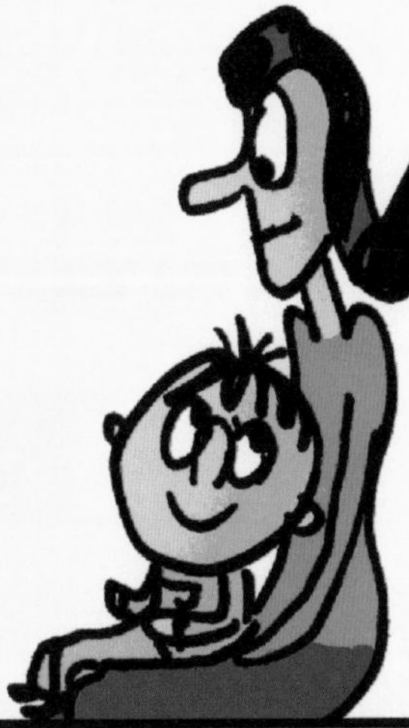

This is my mom.
Great lady.
VERY patient.

Between her and my dad, she's the smart one. That's what she tells me, anyway.

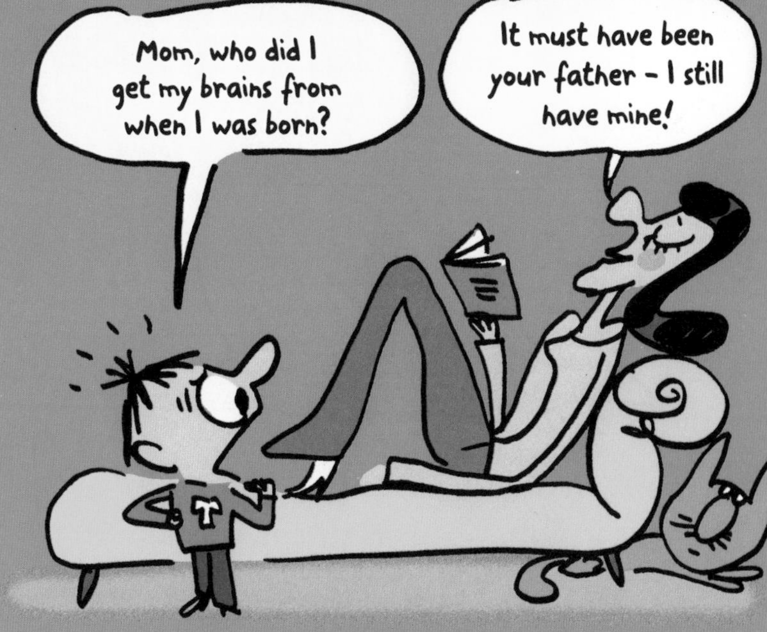
Mom, who did I get my brains from when I was born?
It must have been your father – I still have mine!

My mom is kind when she needs to be, and she's stern when she has to be. I won't say I like her better than my dad, because that's not fair. But I will say she's the best mom I have, and like any good mom, she really looks out for me.

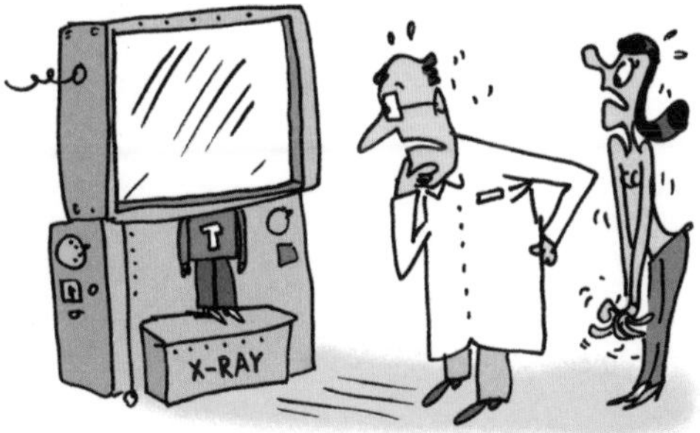
X-RAY

Well, doctor? What do you see?

Nothing . . .

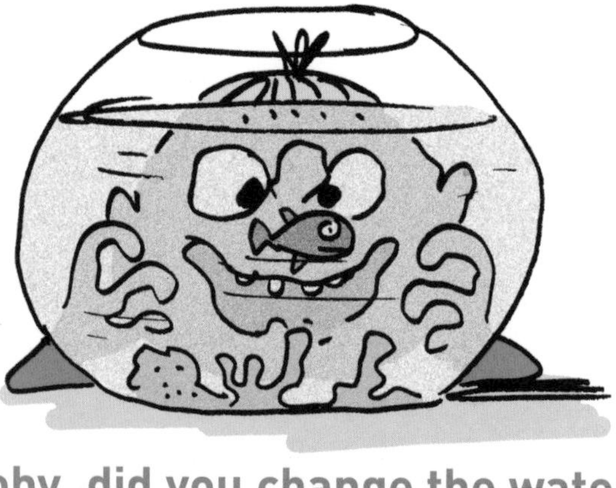

Toby, did you change the water in your goldfish tank?

Not yet, Mom. He hasn't finished what he's got!

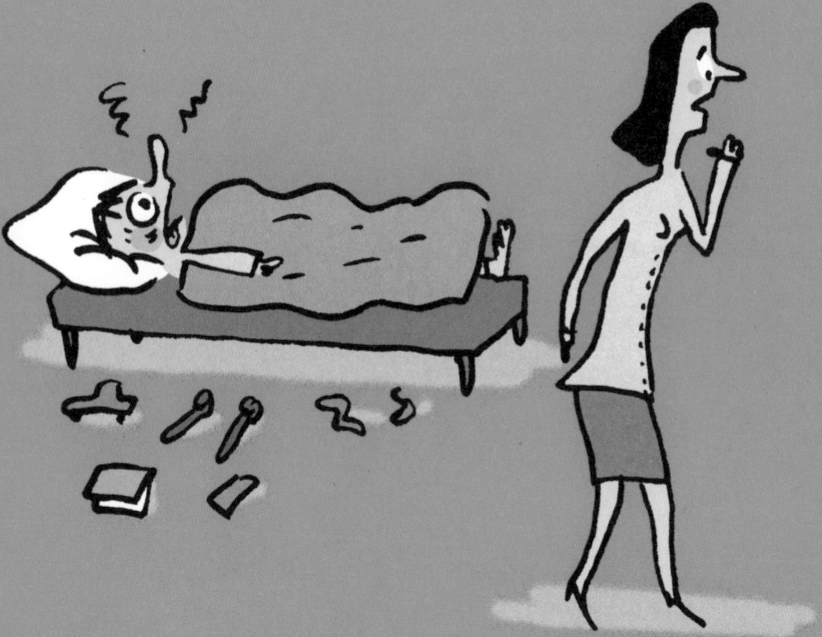

Toby says he has a cold.
I think we should call the doctor.

FORGET IT!

He says that at least once a week.

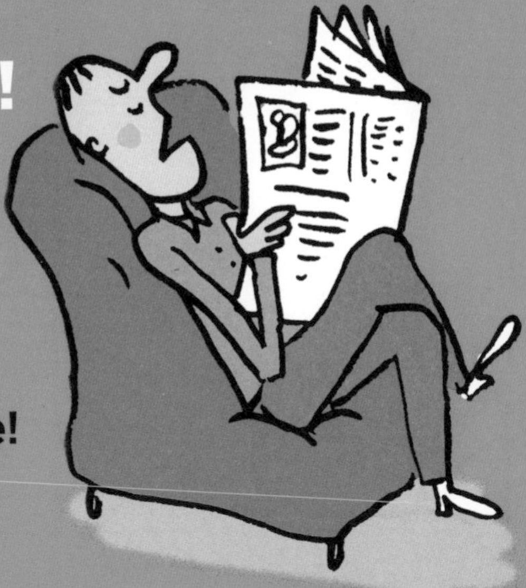

Yes, but he's never said it on a SUNDAY before!

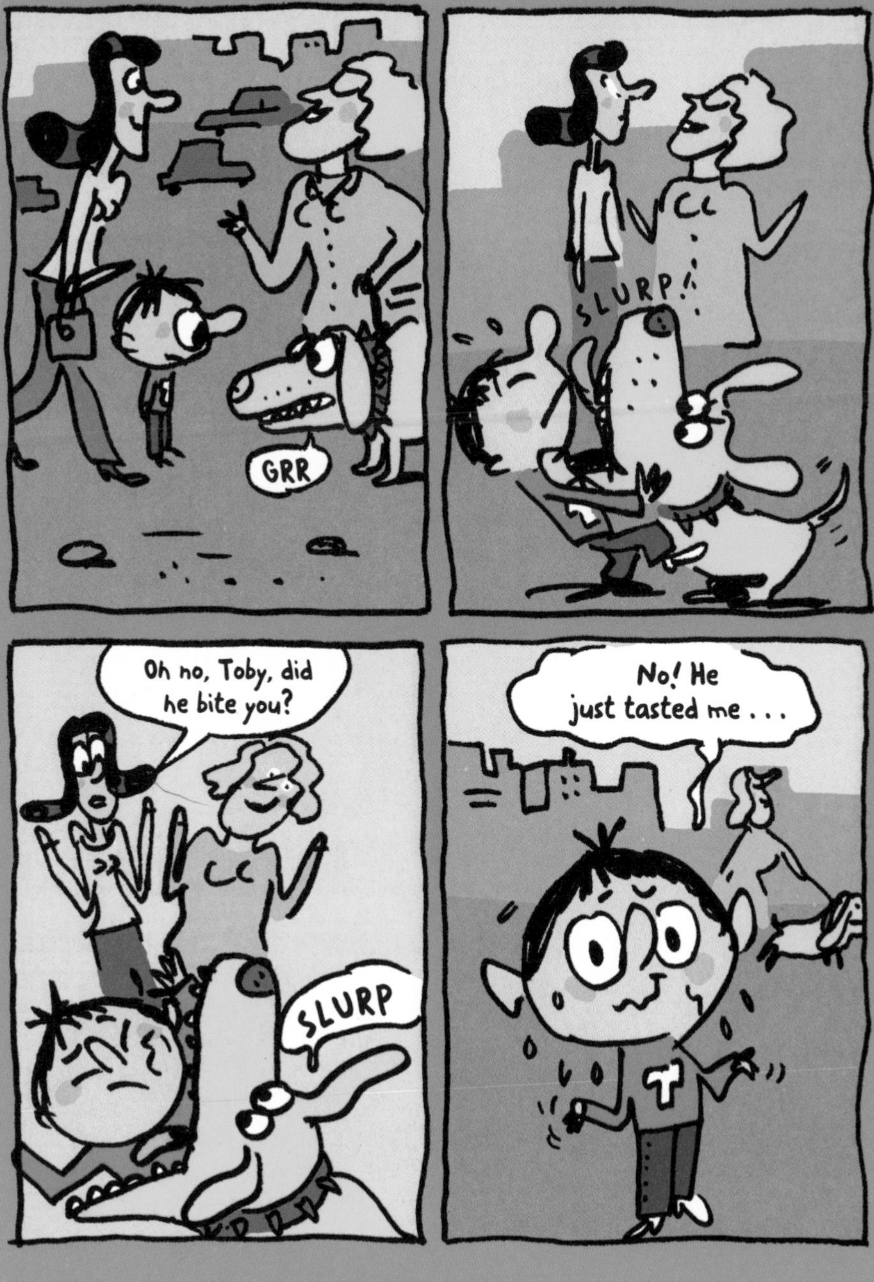
GRR
SLURP!
Oh no, Toby, did he bite you?
SLURP
No! He just tasted me . . .

To tell you the truth, I can be a **REAL** handful. I'm not the easiest kid to control.

I don't always do what I'm told.

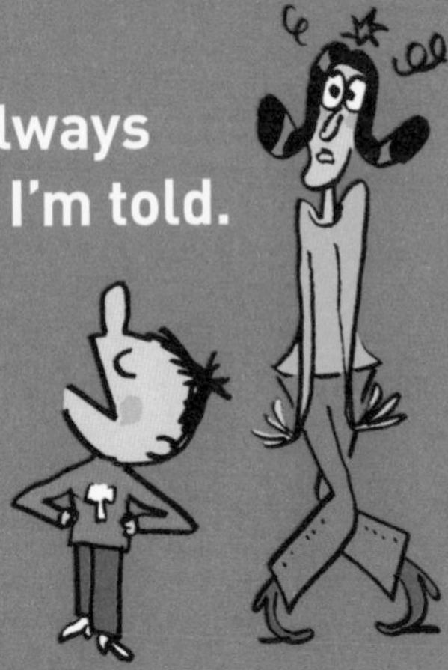

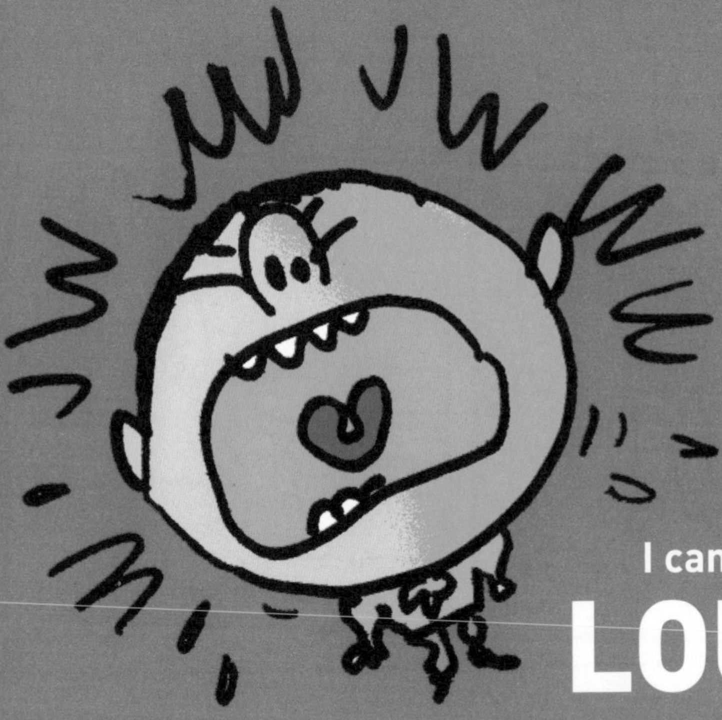

I can get

LOUD.

And stubborn.

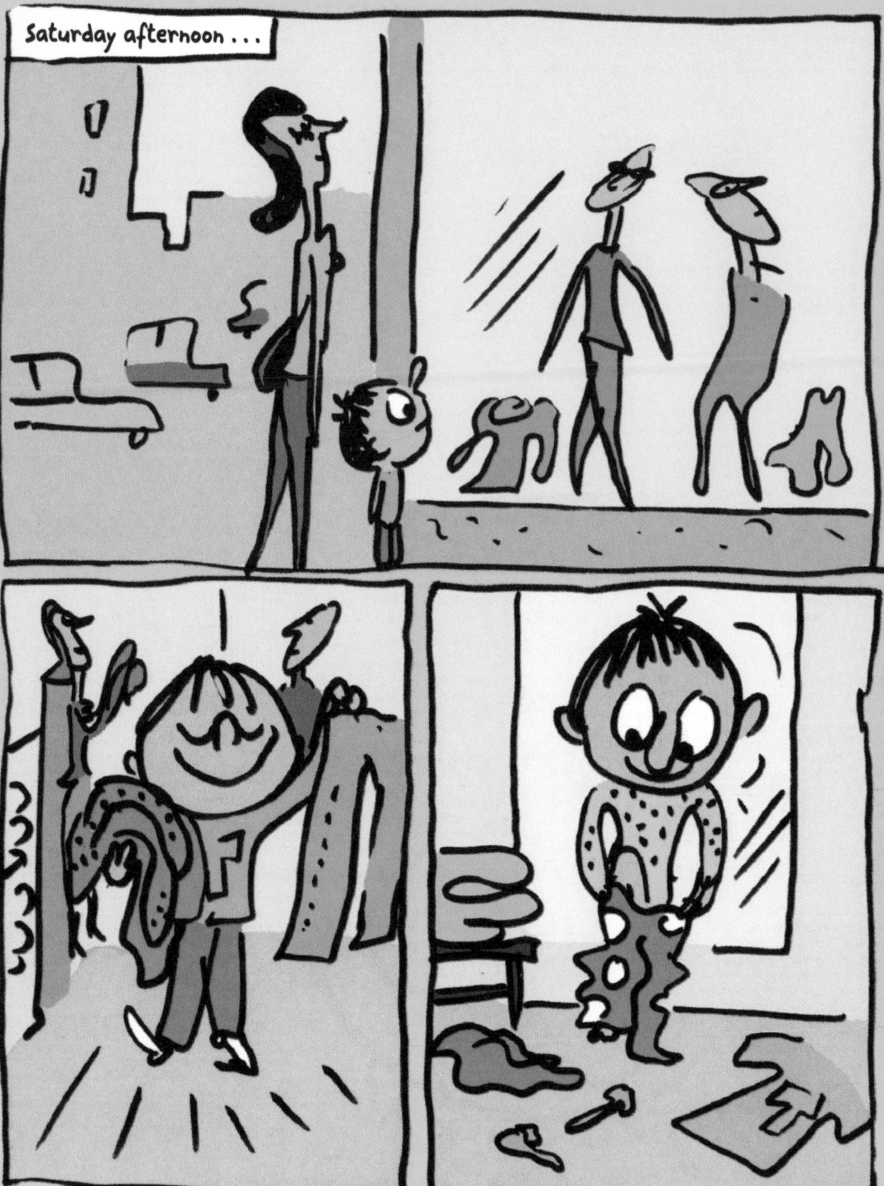
Saturday afternoon . . .

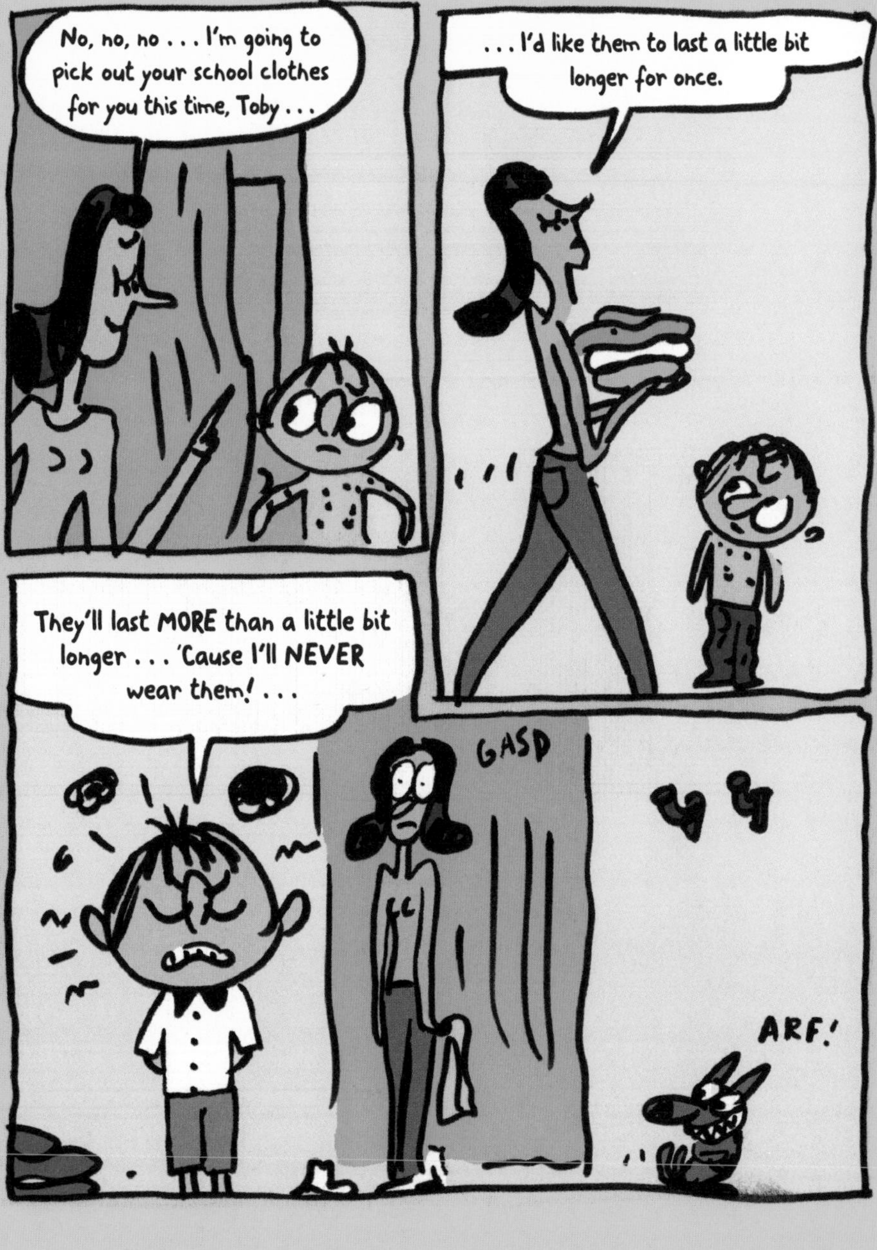
No, no, no . . . I'm going to pick out your school clothes for you this time, Toby . . .
. . . I'd like them to last a little bit longer for once.
They'll last MORE than a little bit longer . . . 'Cause I'll NEVER wear them! . . .
GASP
ARF!

AND I CAN MAKE A
REAL

MESS!

But I'm not naughty all the time. Sometimes I'm downright helpful and nice!

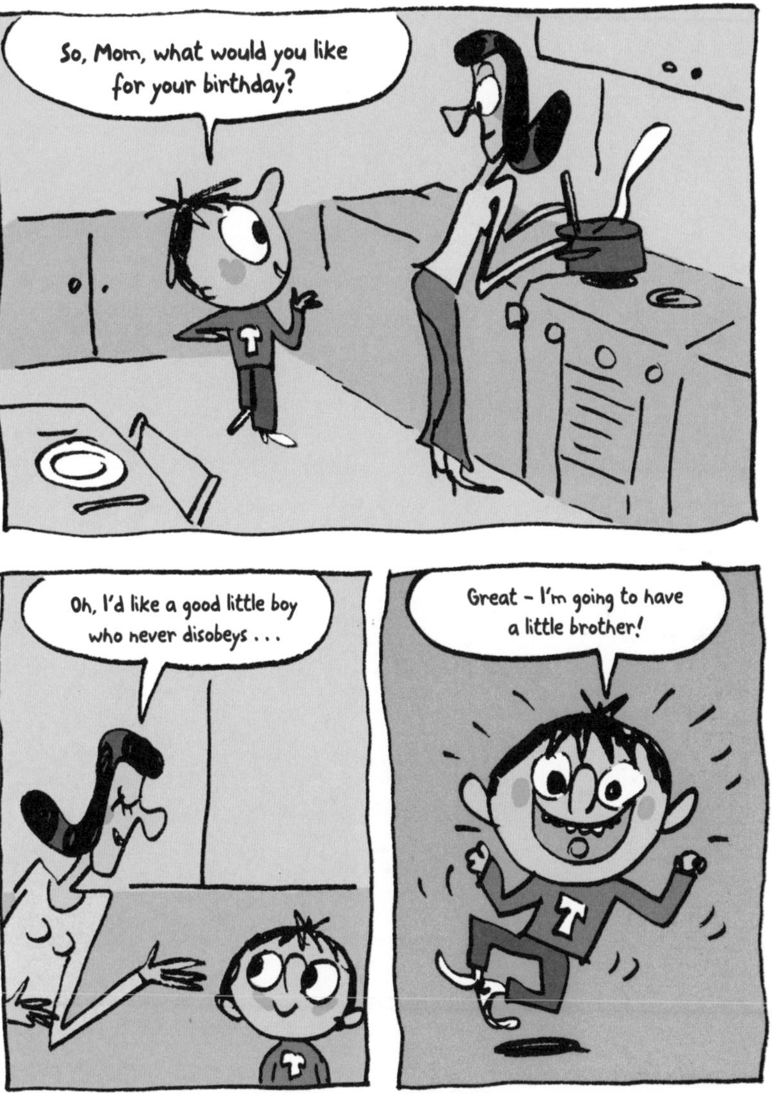
So, Mom, what would you like for your birthday?
Oh, I'd like a good little boy who never disobeys . . .
Great – I'm going to have a little brother!

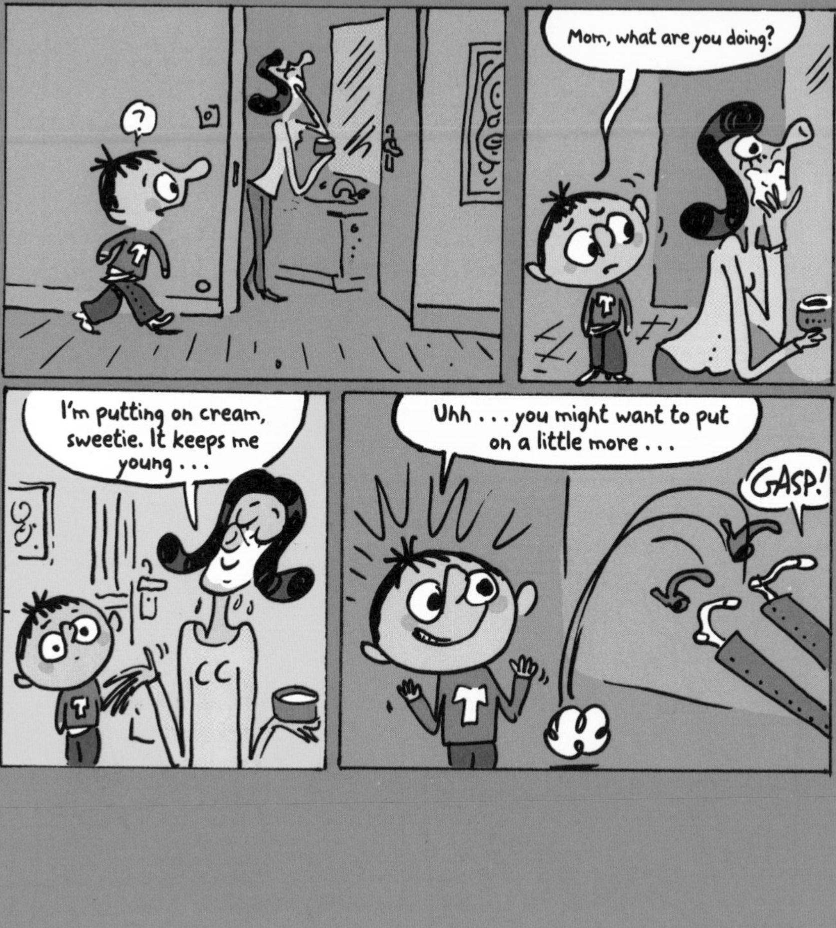
?
Mom, what are you doing?
I'm putting on cream, sweetie. It keeps me young . . .
Uhh . . . you might want to put on a little more . . .
GASP!

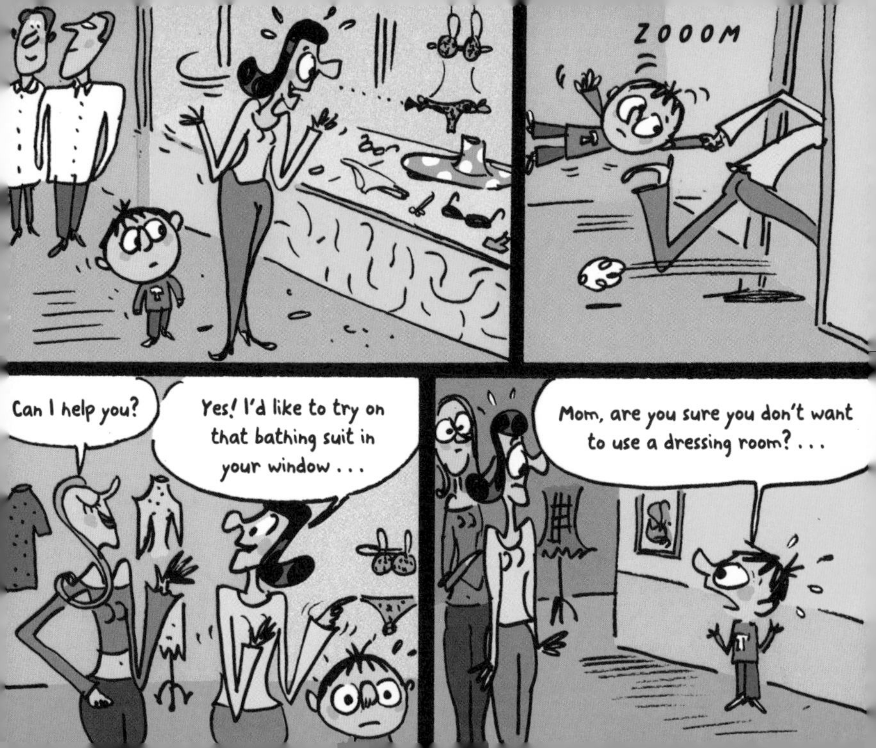
ZOOOM
Can I help you?
Yes! I'd like to try on that bathing suit in your window . . .
Mom, are you sure you don't want to use a dressing room? . . .

And this is my dad.

He's probably not as smart as my mom. He doesn't have her manners, or have as much patience, or always know what's going on around here. But he's a GREAT guy.

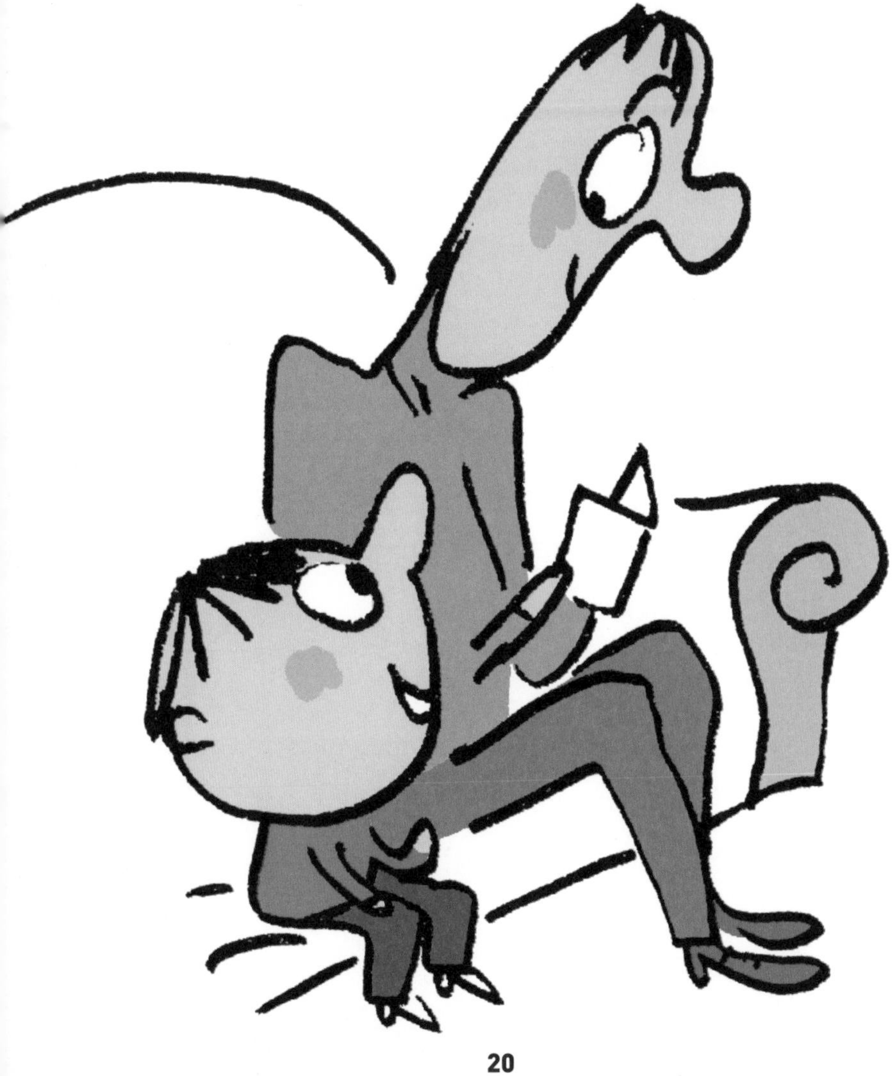

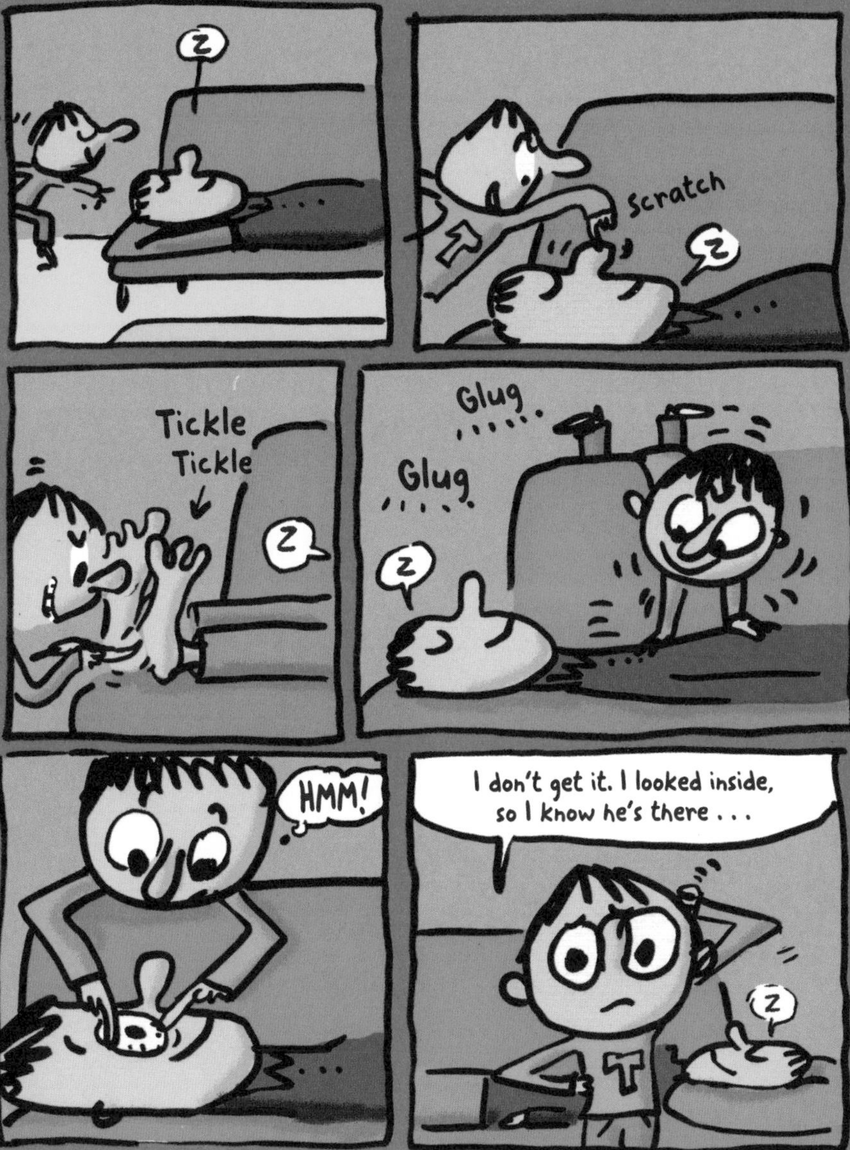
Z
Scratch
Z
Tickle
Tickle
Z
Glug
Glug
Z
HMM!
I don't get it. I looked inside, so I know he's there . . .
Z

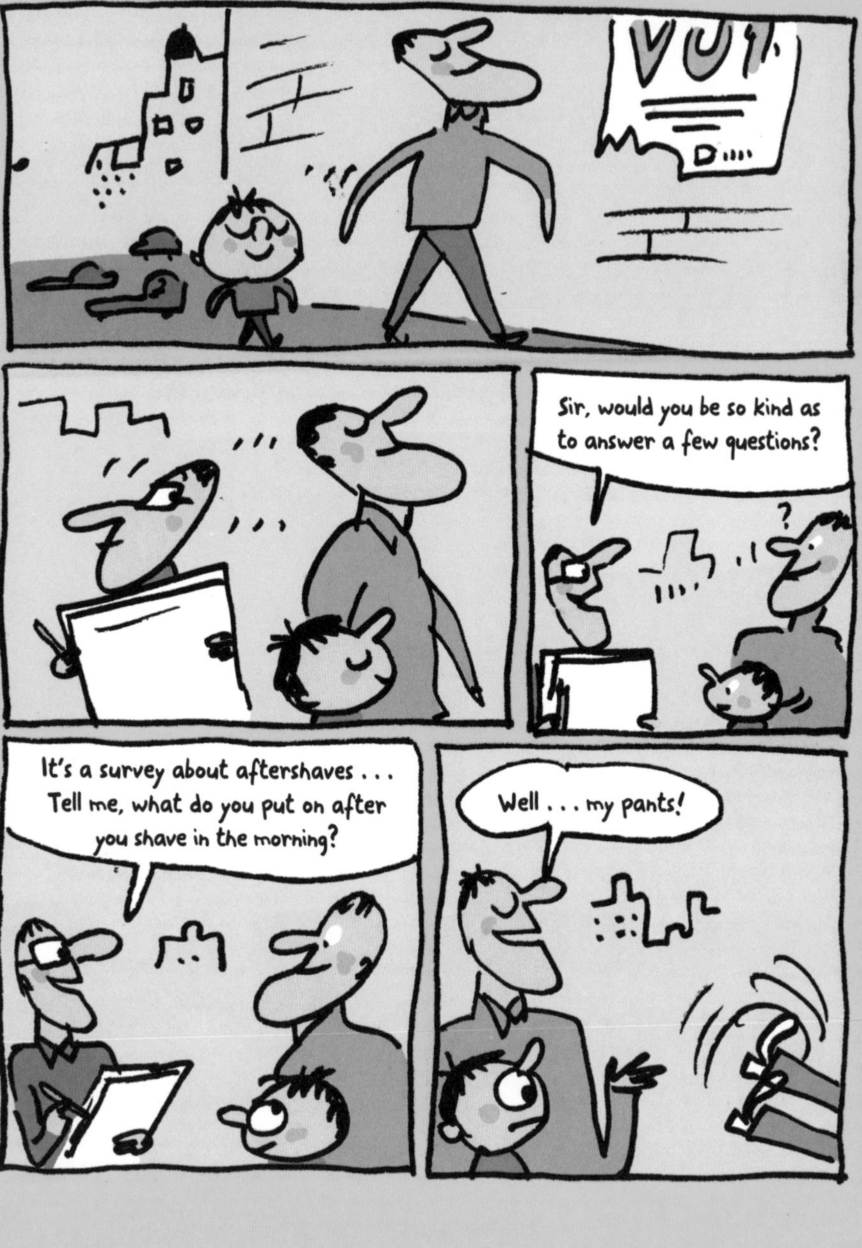
Sir, would you be so kind as to answer a few questions?
It's a survey about aftershaves . . . Tell me, what do you put on after you shave in the morning?
Well . . . my pants!

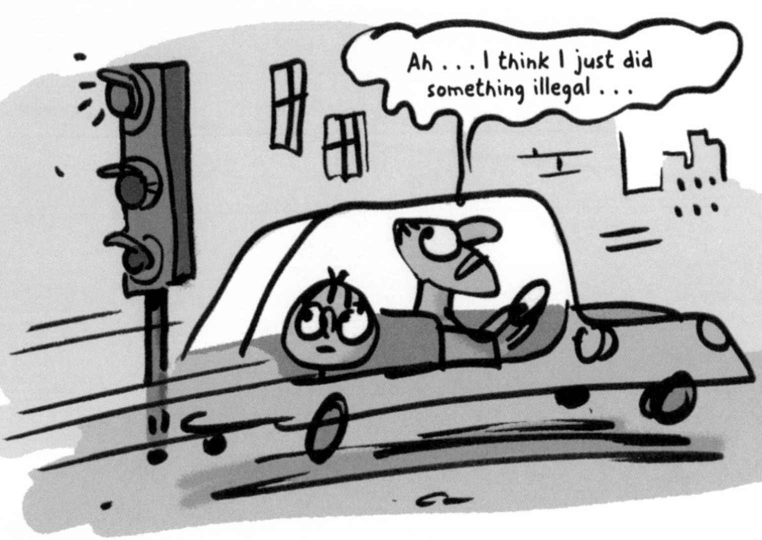
Ah . . . I think I just did something illegal . . .

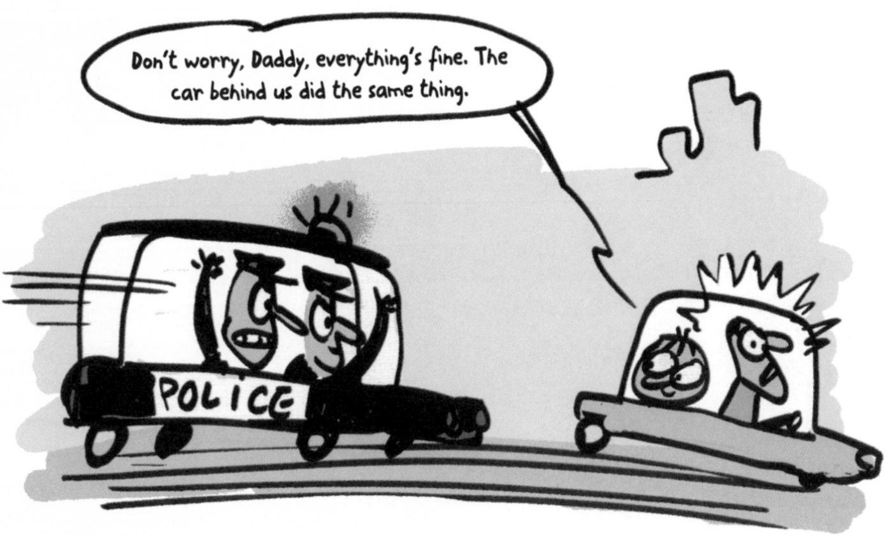
Don't worry, Daddy, everything's fine. The car behind us did the same thing.
POLICE

Now and again he gets mad at me. It's not that he has a short temper. It's just that he makes it so **EASY** for me to get under his skin!

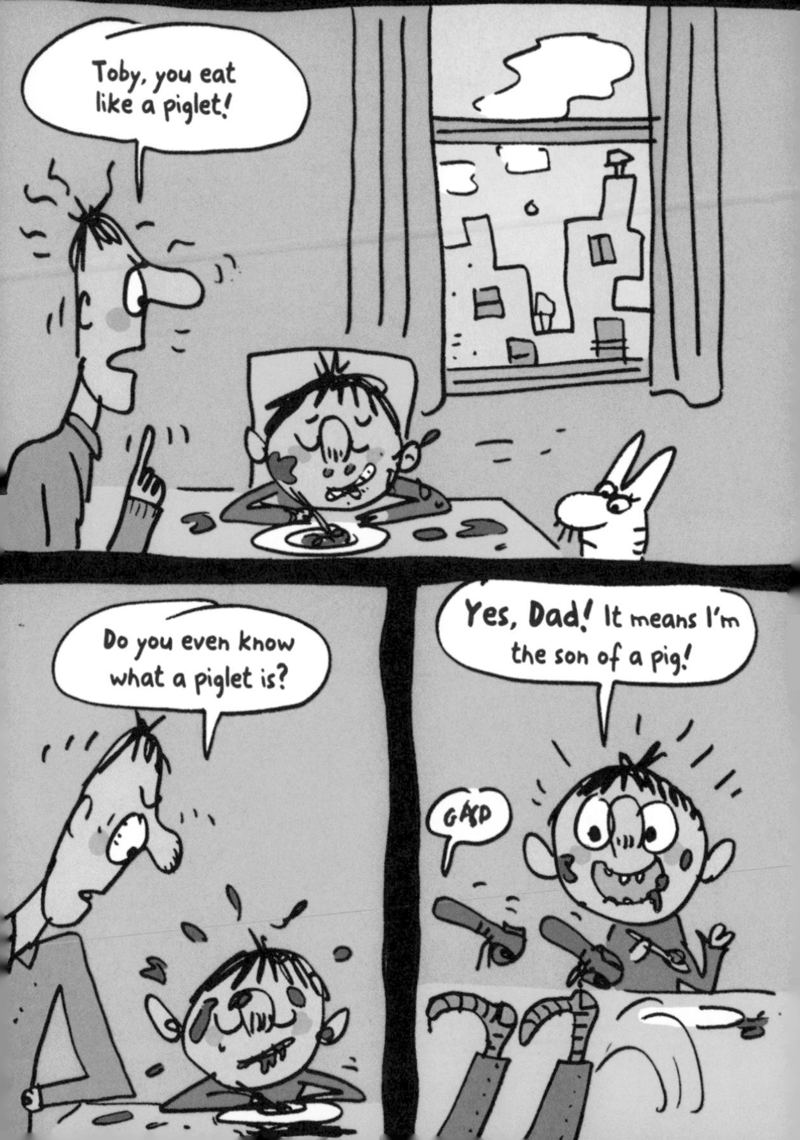
Toby, you eat like a piglet!
Do you even know what a piglet is?
Yes, Dad! It means I'm the son of a pig!
GASP

But the great thing about my dad is that he **ALWAYS** has time for me. And that's the best, because when I'm not in school . . .

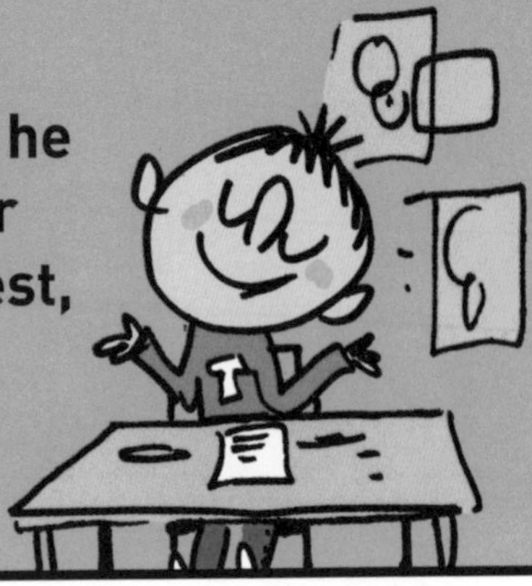

. . . goofing off . . .

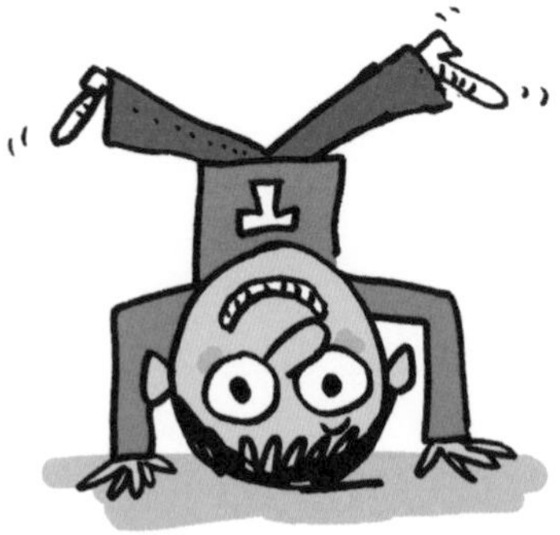

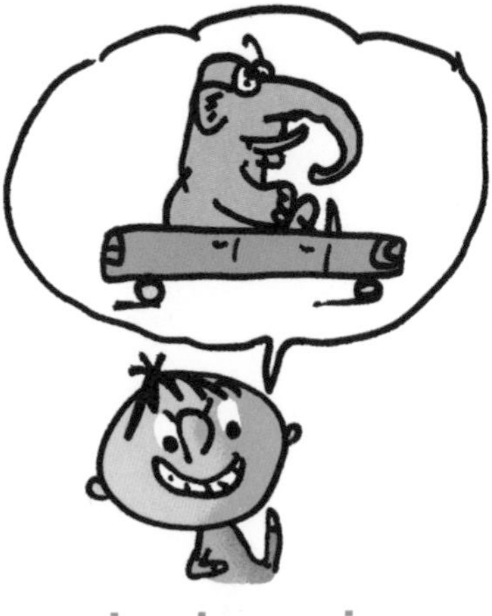

. . . daydreaming . . .

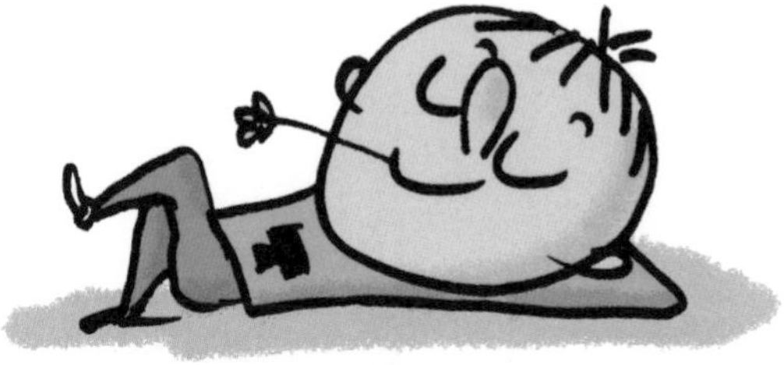

. . . or just sitting around doing **NOTHING**, time is pretty much all I've got!

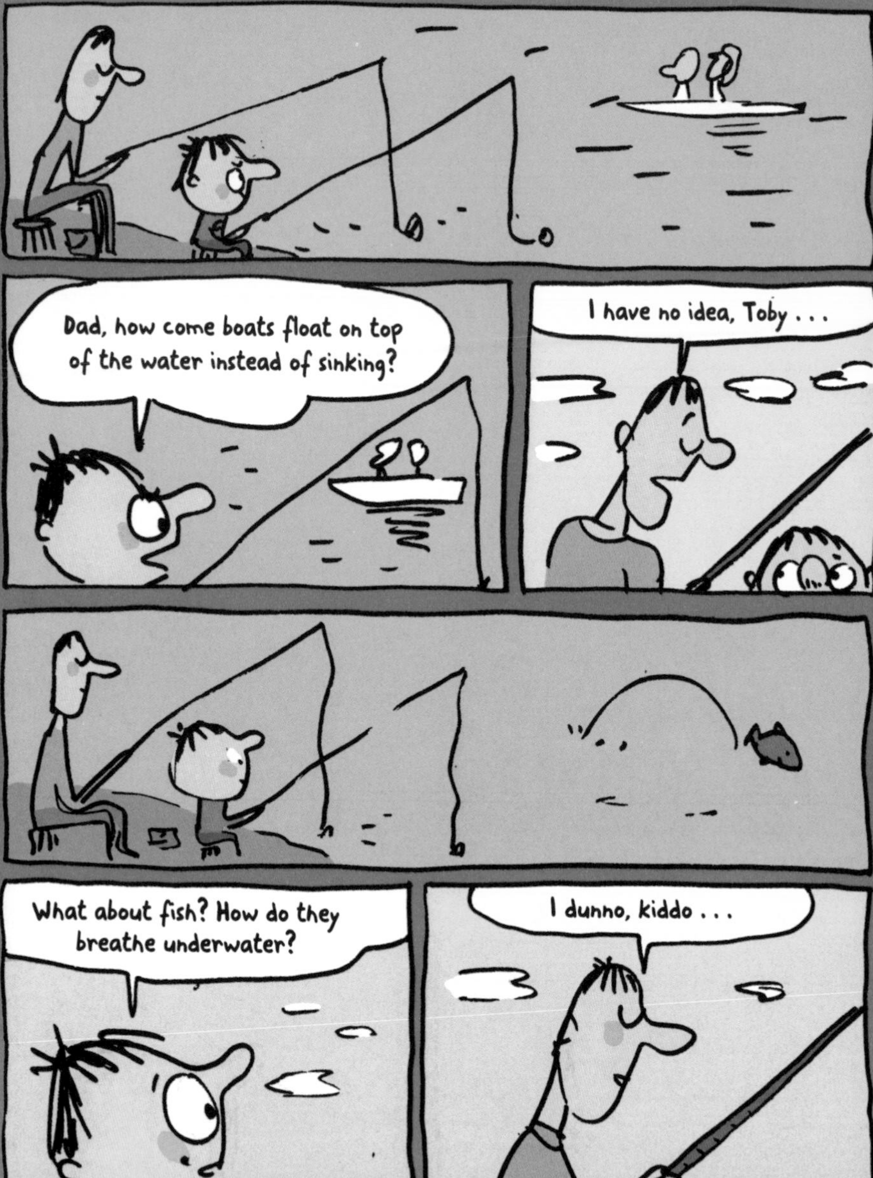
Dad, how come boats float on top of the water instead of sinking?
I have no idea, Toby . . .
What about fish? How do they breathe underwater?
I dunno, kiddo . . .

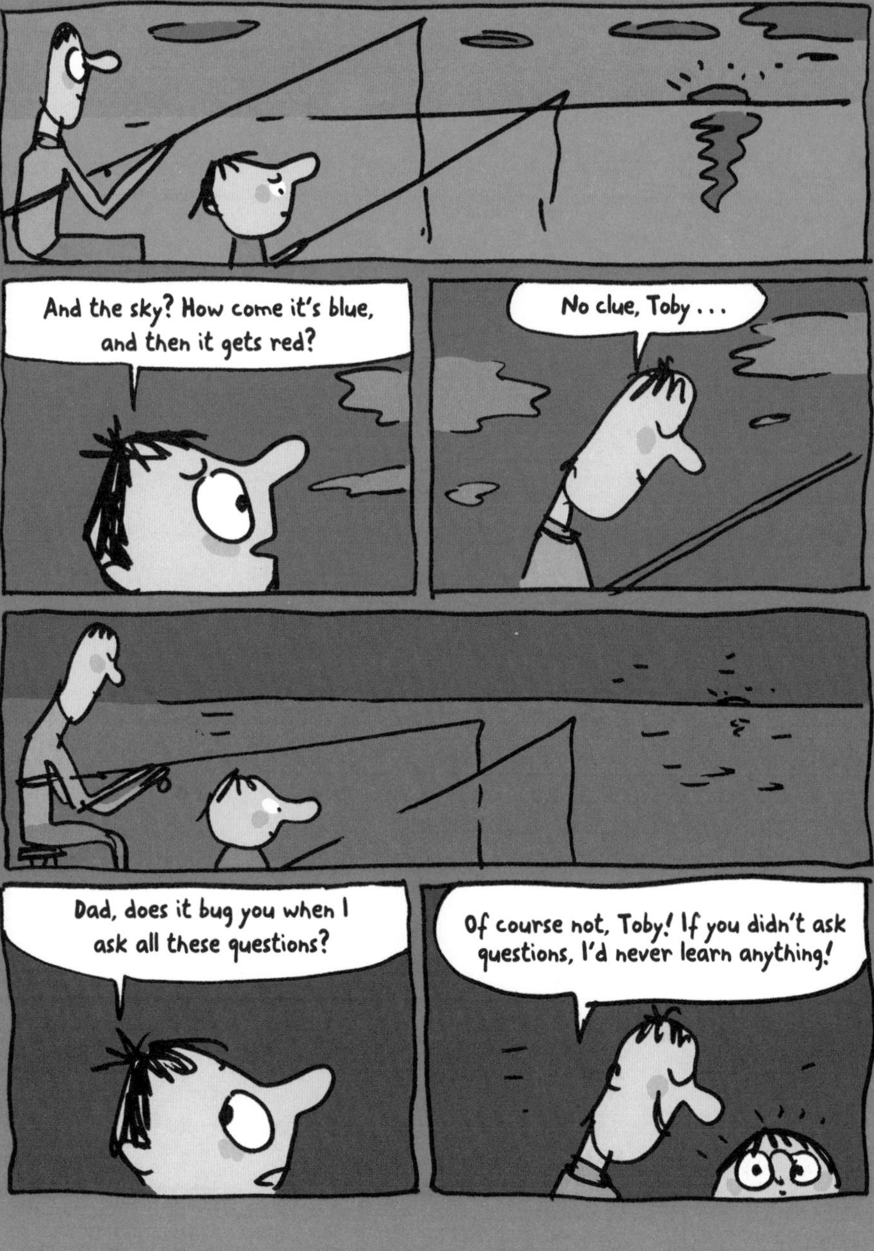
And the sky? How come it's blue, and then it gets red?
No clue, Toby . . .
Dad, does it bug you when I ask all these questions?
Of course not, Toby! If you didn't ask questions, I'd never learn anything!

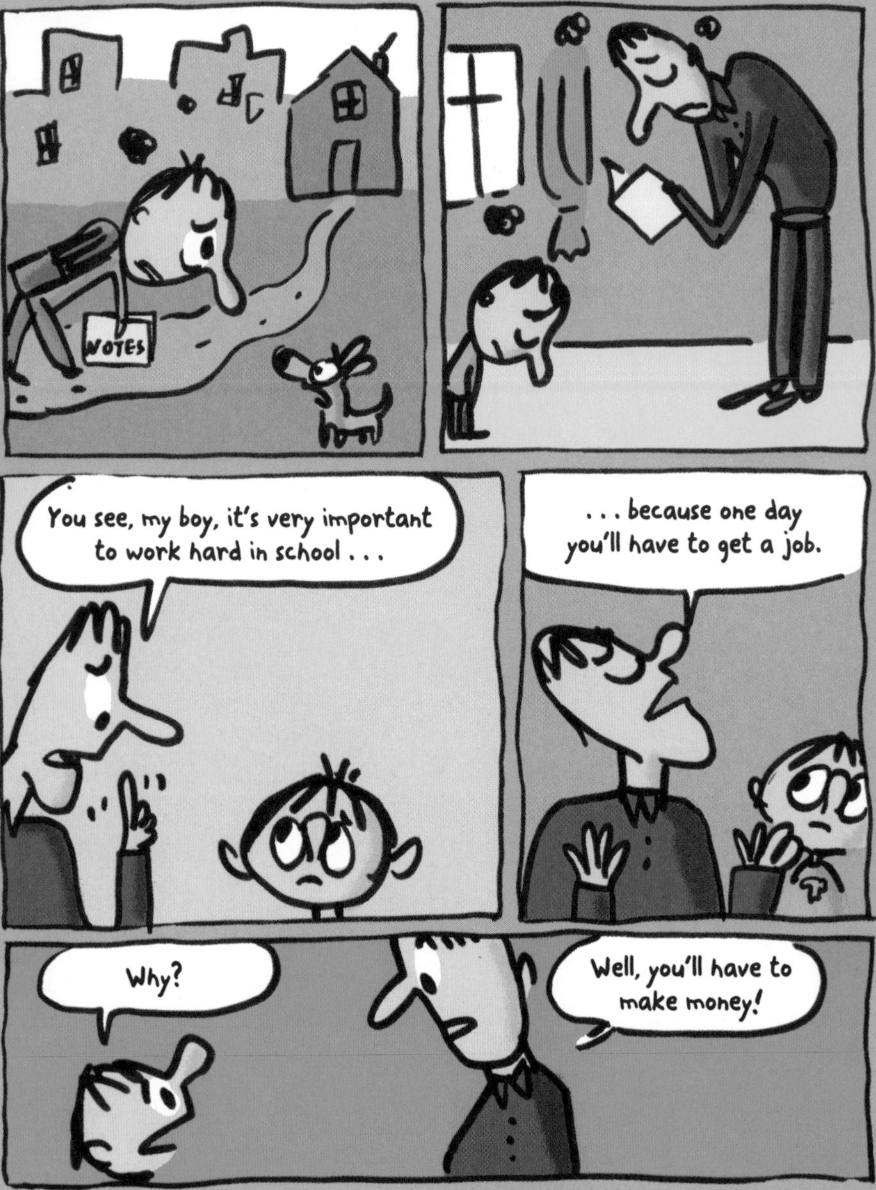
NOTES
You see, my boy, it's very important to work hard in school . . .
. . . because one day you'll have to get a job.
Why?
Well, you'll have to make money!

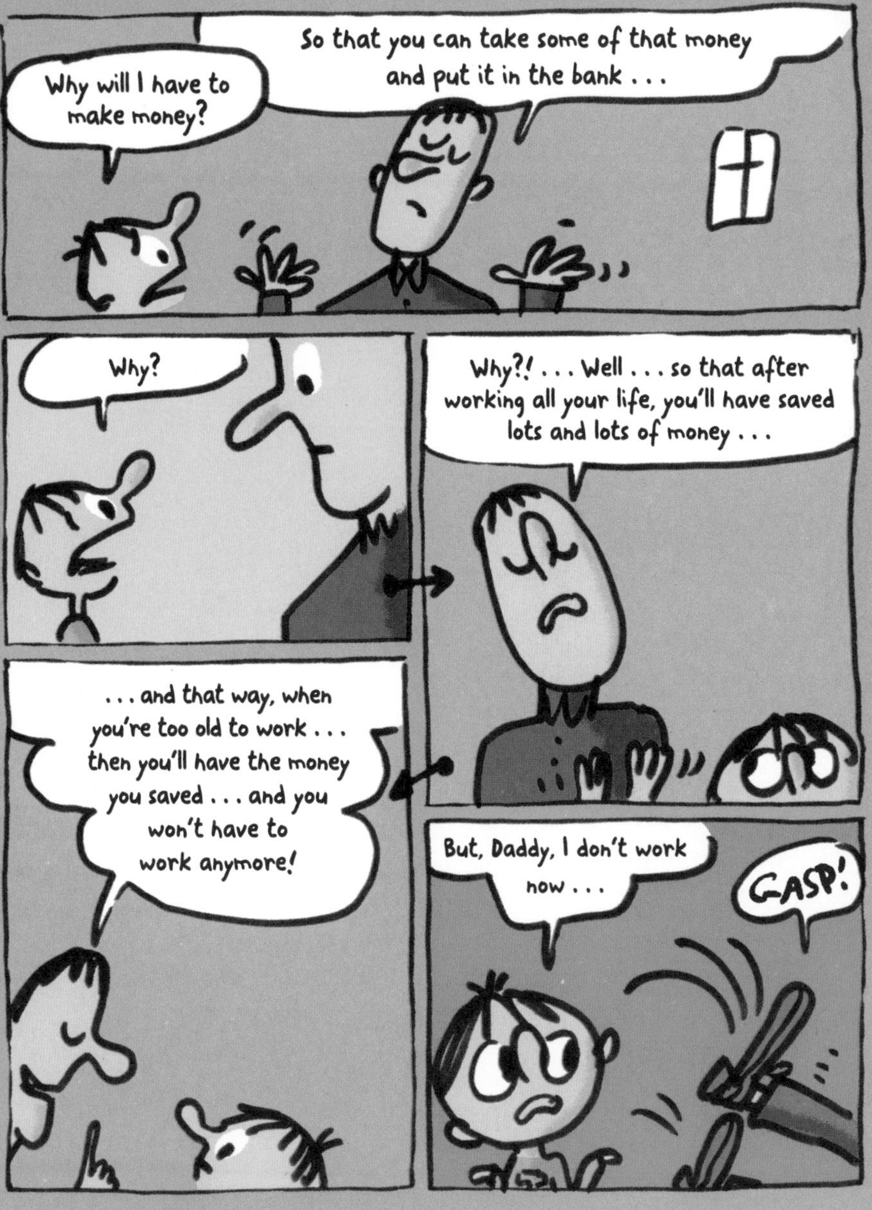
Why will I have to make money?
So that you can take some of that money and put it in the bank . . .
Why?
Why?! . . . Well . . . so that after working all your life, you'll have saved lots and lots of money . . .
. . . and that way, when you're too old to work . . . then you'll have the money you saved . . . and you won't have to work anymore!
But, Daddy, I don't work now . . .
GASP!

And finally there's Zaza, my sister.

**Zaza is her nickname.
Her real name is Suzy, but mom calls
her Zaza because it sounds French.**

(Mom loves **ANYTHING** French.)

We get along okay, but sometimes **ZAZA CAN BE A PAIN.** She says I never give her anything. Like my toys, or extra cake, or one of my cookies.

THAT'S NOT EVEN TRUE!

Just last month I gave her a cold!

And just the other night I gave her a **GOOD SCARE!**

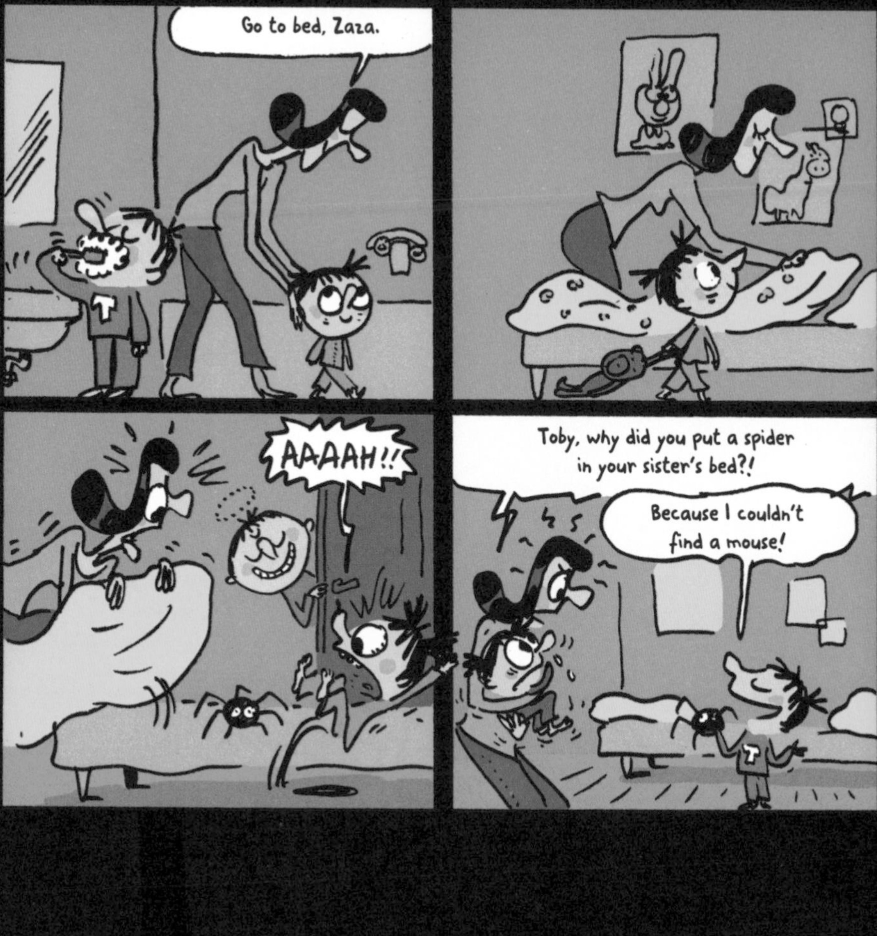

Go to bed, Zaza.
AAAAH!!
Toby, why did you put a spider in your sister's bed?!
Because I couldn't find a mouse!

One thing is for sure. Zaza doesn't know when to stop talking, **ESPECIALLY** when her blabber mouth gets me in trouble.

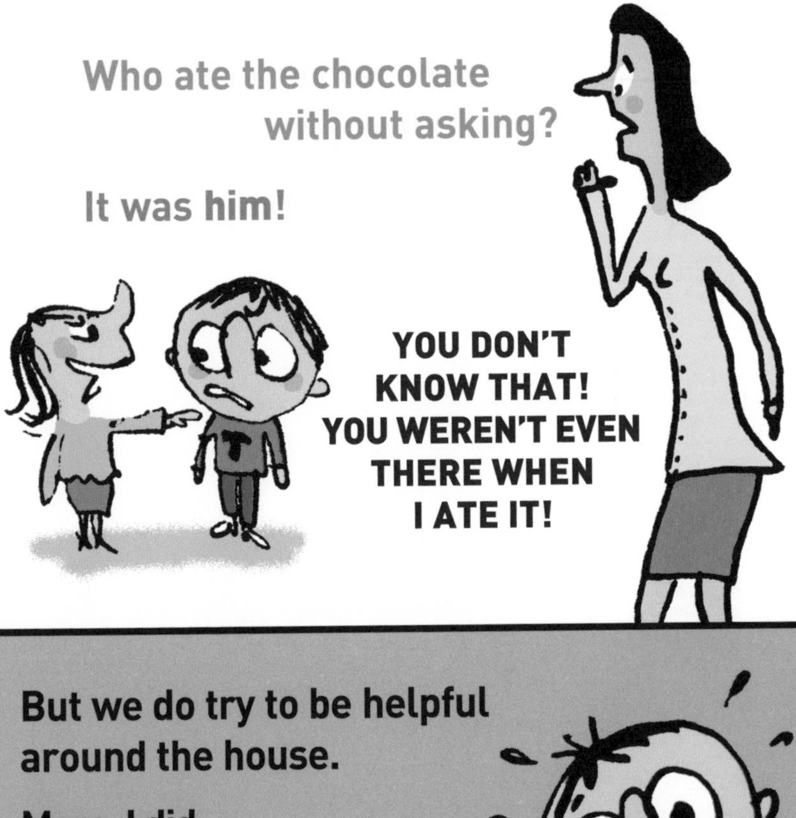
Who ate the chocolate without asking?
It was **him**!
YOU DON'T KNOW THAT! YOU WEREN'T EVEN THERE WHEN I ATE IT!

But we do try to be helpful around the house.

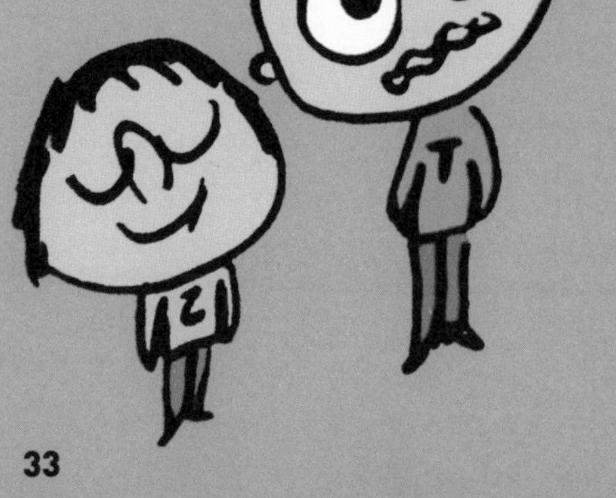
Mom, I did the dishes! . . .
That's great, Toby. What about you, Zaza?
I picked up the broken pieces . . .

You probably want to know more about my day, or what my life is like in general.

OR maybe you want to ride around on the back of a dinosaur shooting lasers out of your fingertips!

(I don't know. I'm not a mind reader!)

ANYWAY, I already told you about my freaky dreams and not wanting to get out of bed in the morning. And you met my pretty okay family. You know, all the normal stuff.

Overall, my life is good. Mostly, I try to make things interesting for myself.

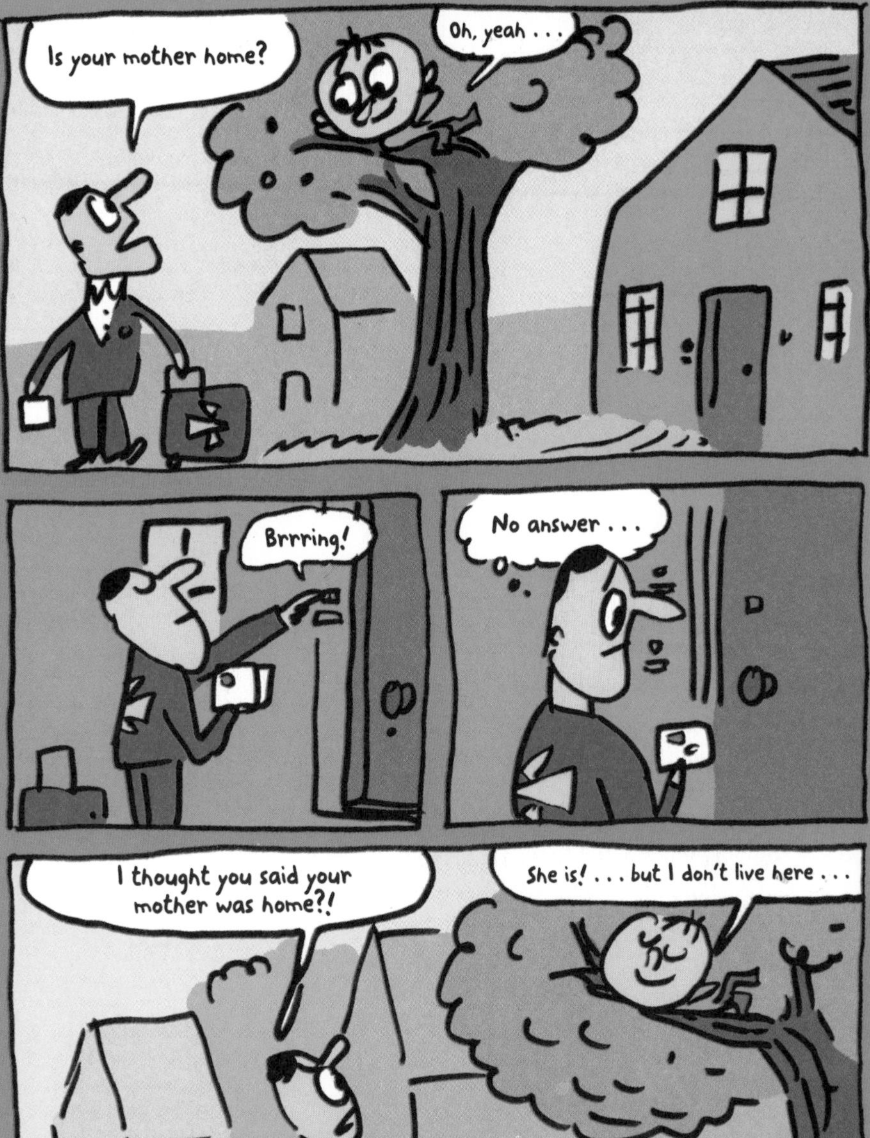
Is your mother home?
Oh, yeah . . .
Brrring!
No answer . . .
I thought you said your mother was home?!
She is! . . . but I don't live here . . .

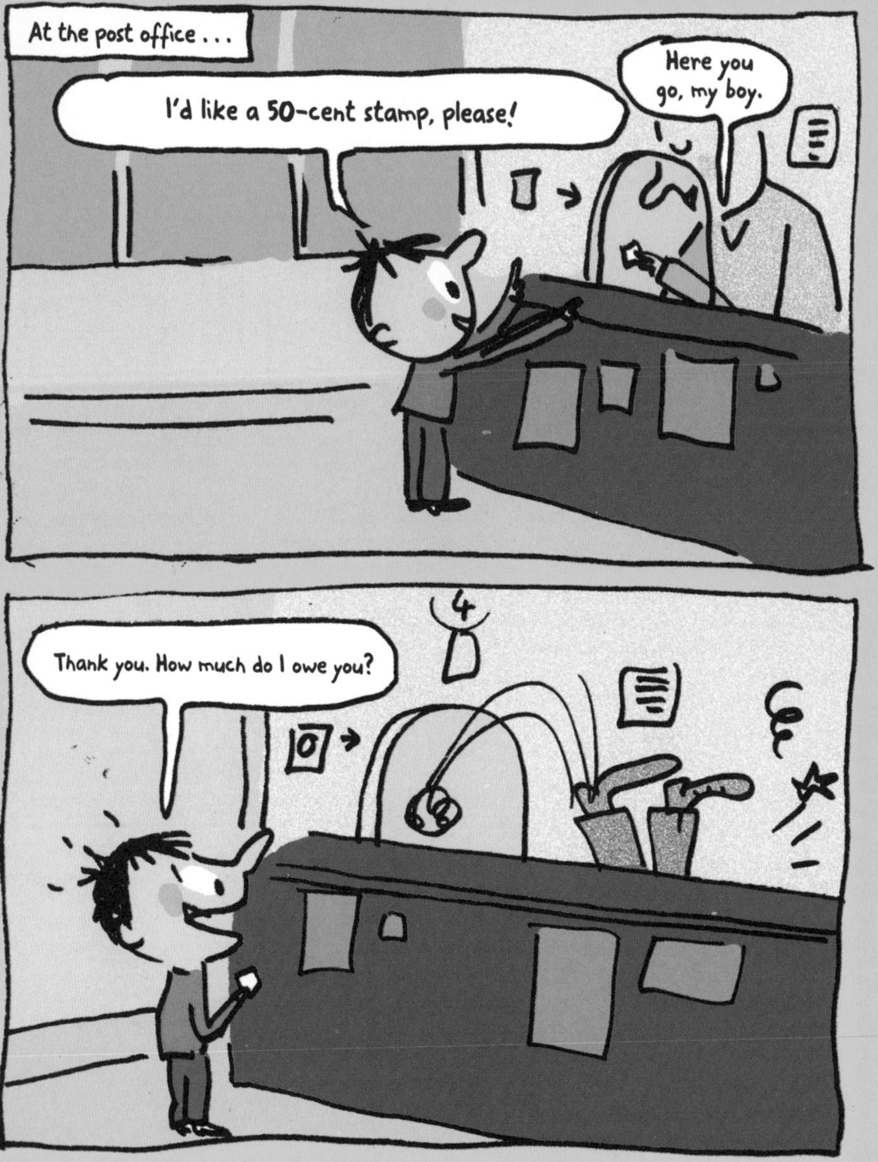
At the post office . . .
I'd like a 50-cent stamp, please!
Here you go, my boy.
Thank you. How much do I owe you?

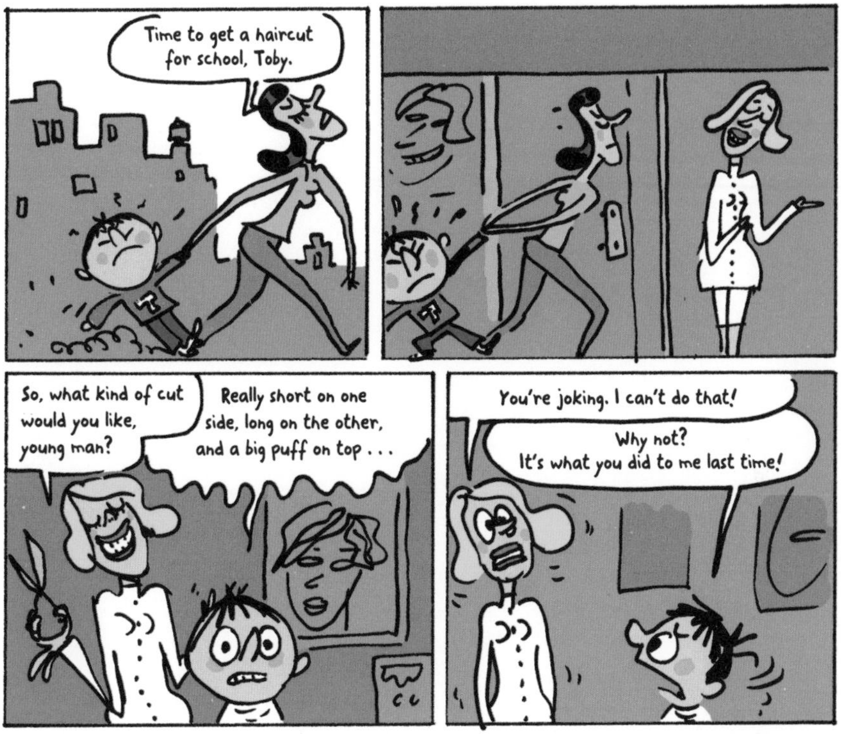
Time to get a haircut for school, Toby.
So, what kind of cut would you like, young man?
Really short on one side, long on the other, and a big puff on top . . .
You're joking. I can't do that!
Why not? It's what you did to me last time!

Mom, Mom! Is it true that when you die, you turn to dust?

Yes, sweetie.

Then come quick! There's a dead person under my bed!

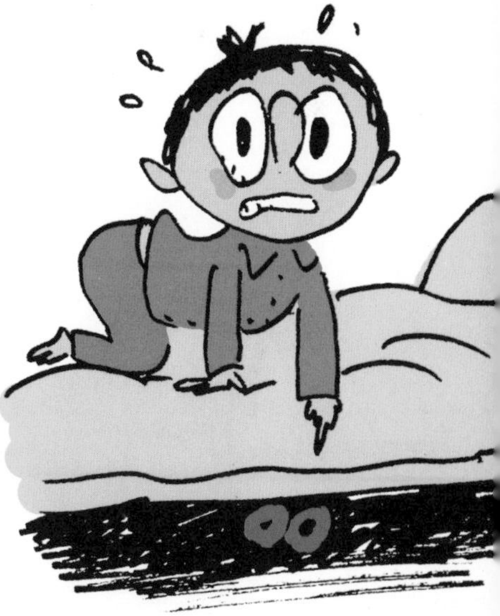

To be honest, though, it's not always easy. It's a busy world out there, full of people going this way and that way. Everyone has their own life. It can be hard to get a person's attention . . .

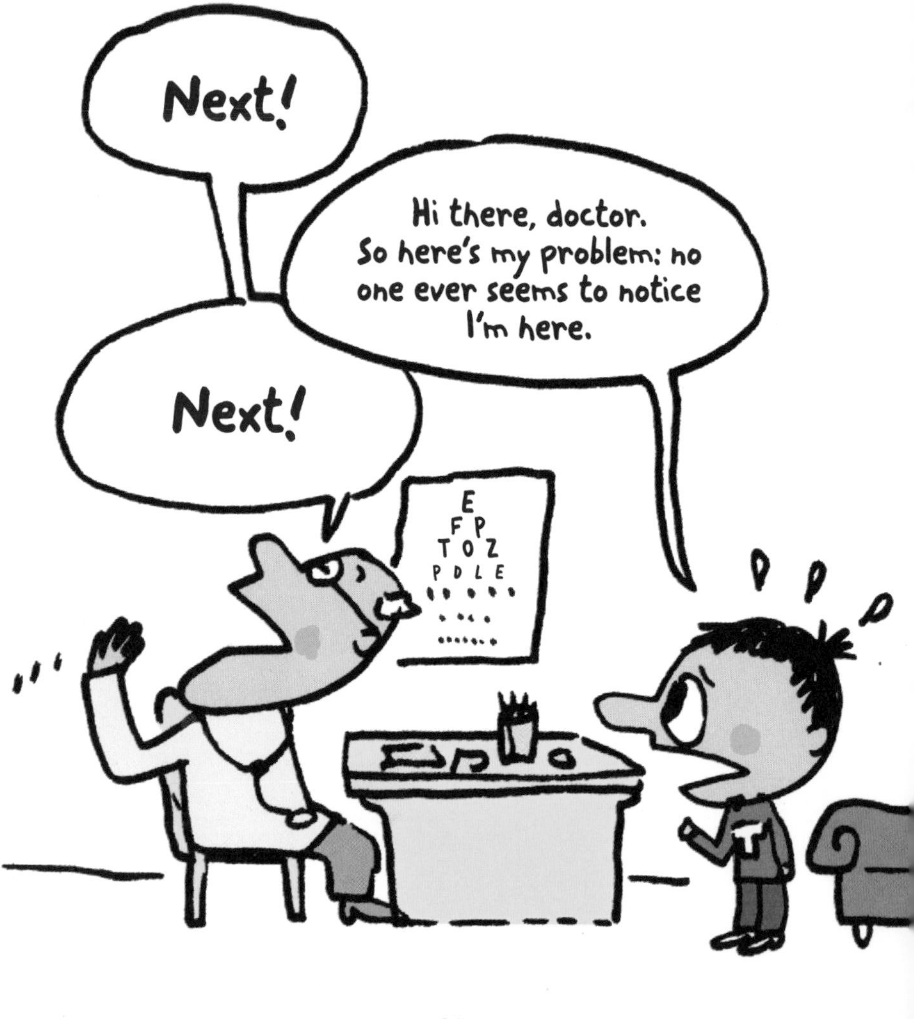
Next!
Next!
Hi there, doctor. So here's my problem: no one ever seems to notice I'm here.
E
F P
T O Z
P D L E

That's when I like to spice things up a bit.

My favorite way to keep things lively is to mess with grown-ups. It really drives them CRAZY! And that always cheers me up!

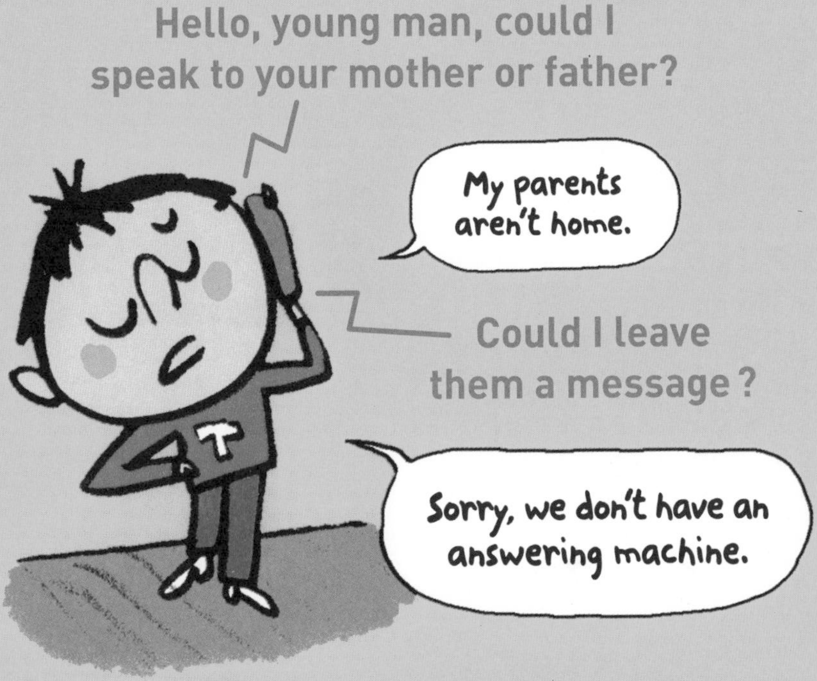
Hello, young man, could I speak to your mother or father?
My parents aren't home.
Could I leave them a message?
Sorry, we don't have an answering machine.

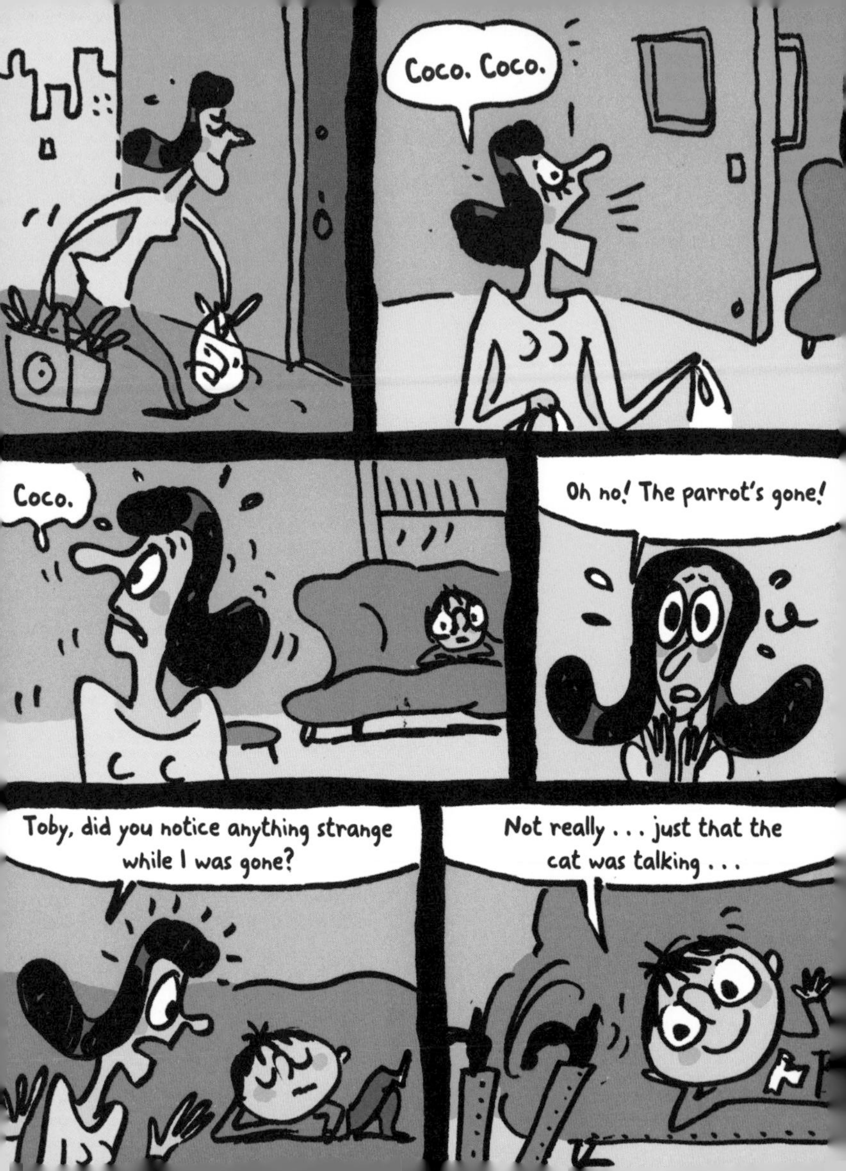
Coco. Coco.
Coco.
Oh no! The parrot's gone!
Toby, did you notice anything strange while I was gone?
Not really . . . just that the cat was talking . . .

But to get the most out of life, you need good friends. And I have some great ones.

My best friend is George.

I've known him all my life. When I'm feeling down, he picks me up. When I need a buddy, he's by my side. When I'm feeling dumb, he makes me feel smart.

(I'm going to tell the truth here, because I respect you too much to lie. George isn't the sharpest crayon in the box.)

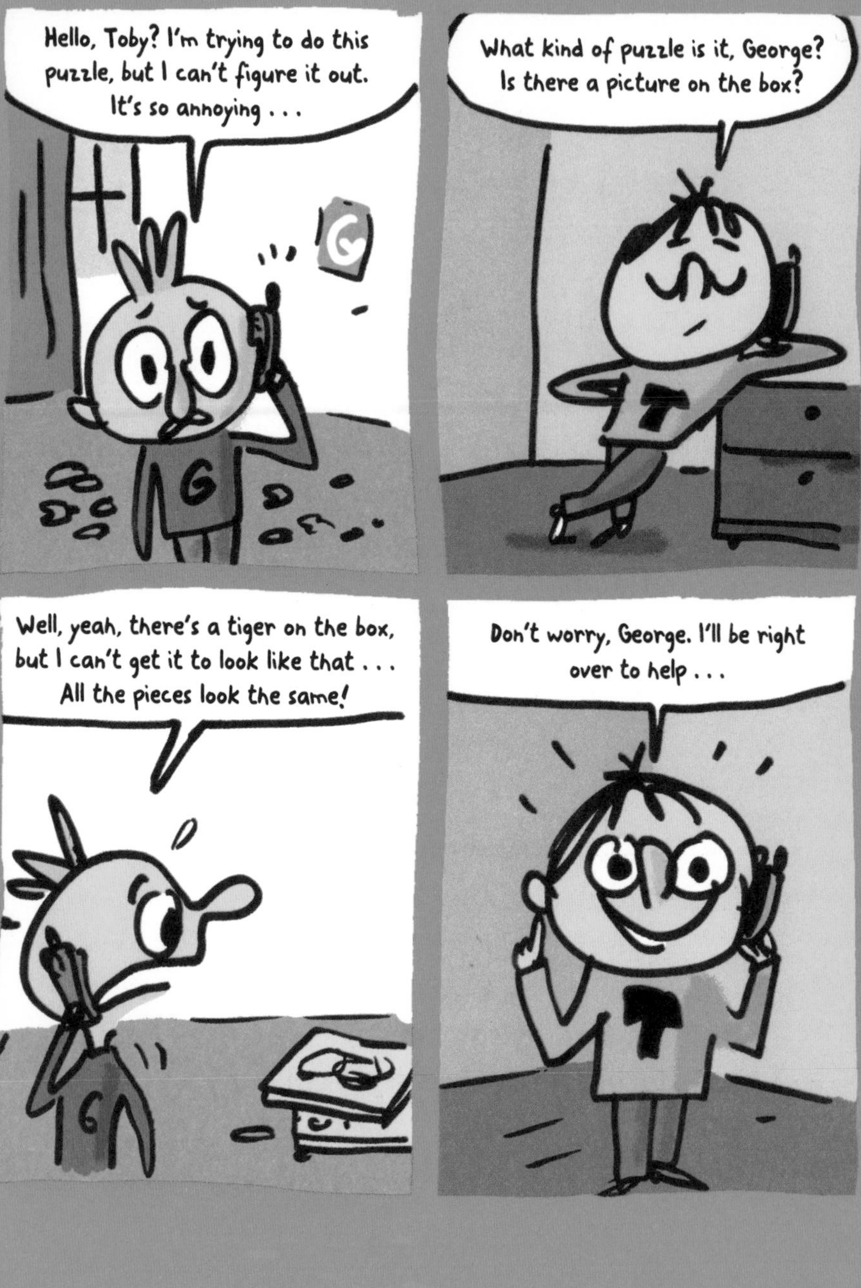
Hello, Toby? I'm trying to do this puzzle, but I can't figure it out. It's so annoying . . .
What kind of puzzle is it, George? Is there a picture on the box?
Well, yeah, there's a tiger on the box, but I can't get it to look like that . . . All the pieces look the same!
Don't worry, George. I'll be right over to help . . .

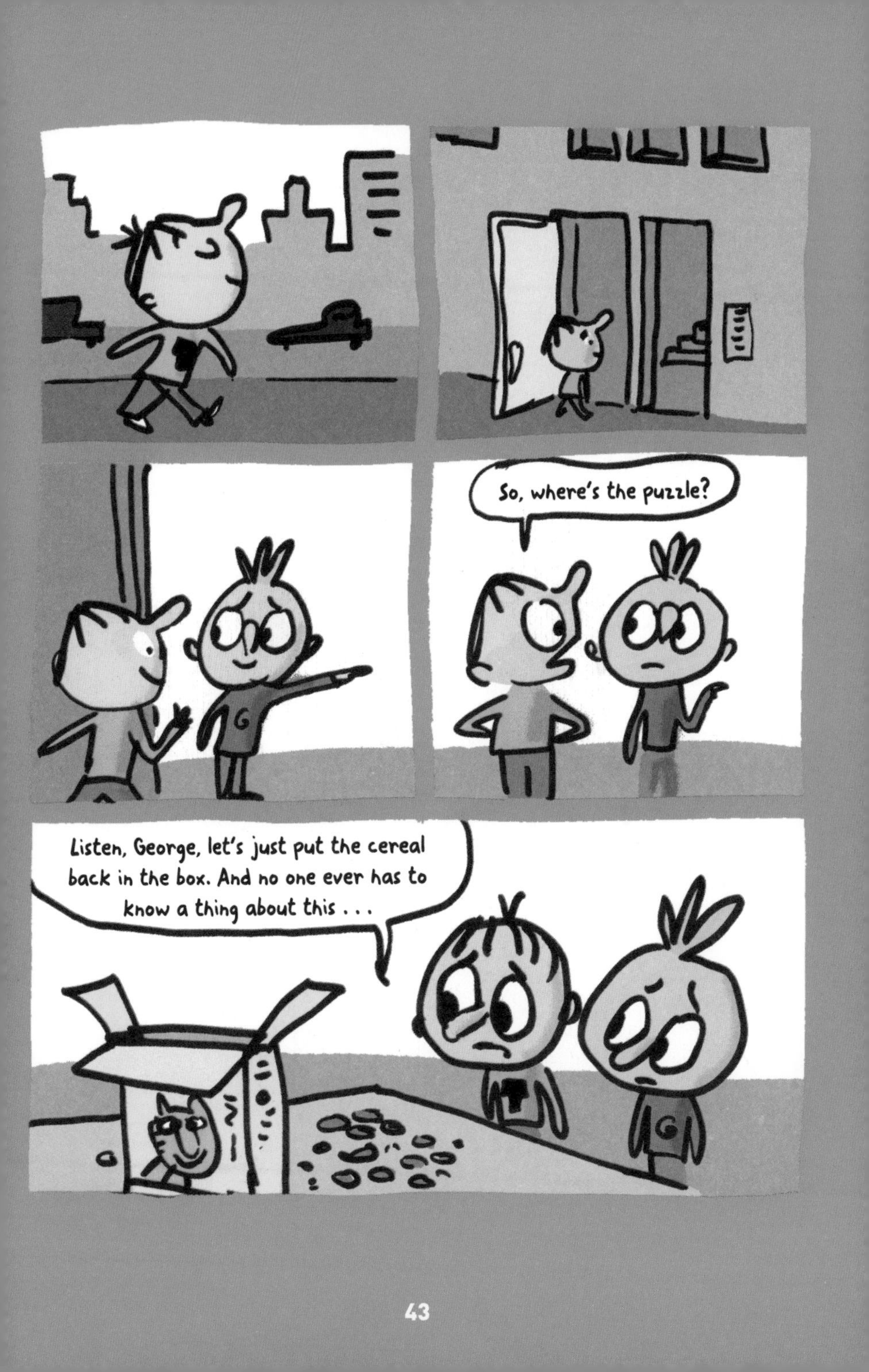
So, where's the puzzle?
Listen, George, let's just put the cereal back in the box. And no one ever has to know a thing about this . . .

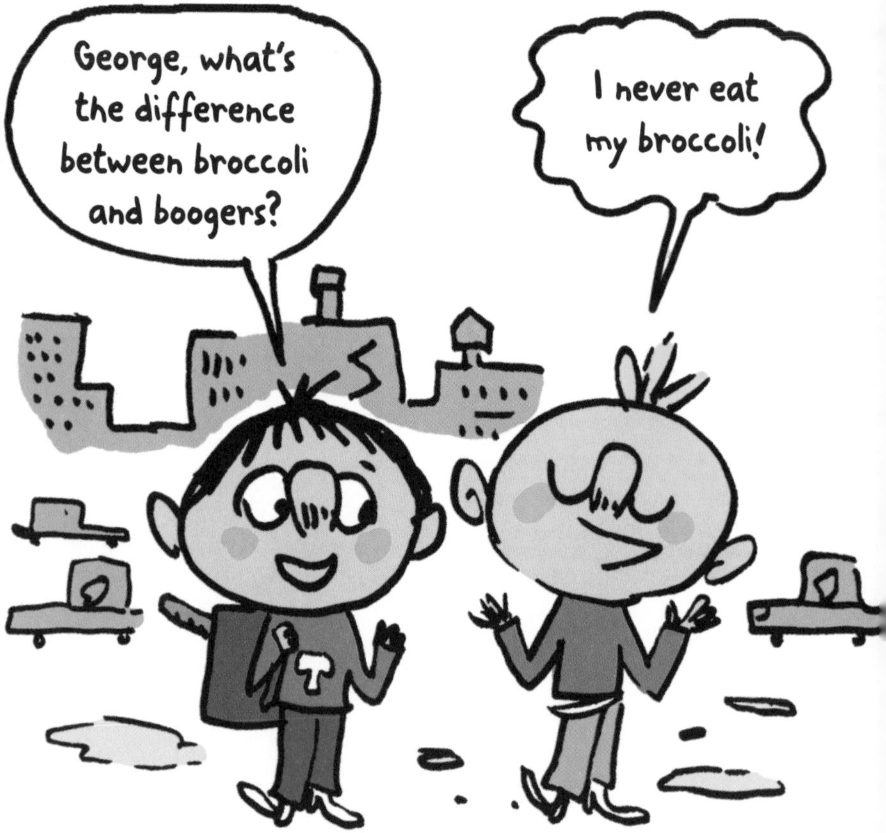
George, what's the difference between broccoli and boogers?
I never eat my broccoli!

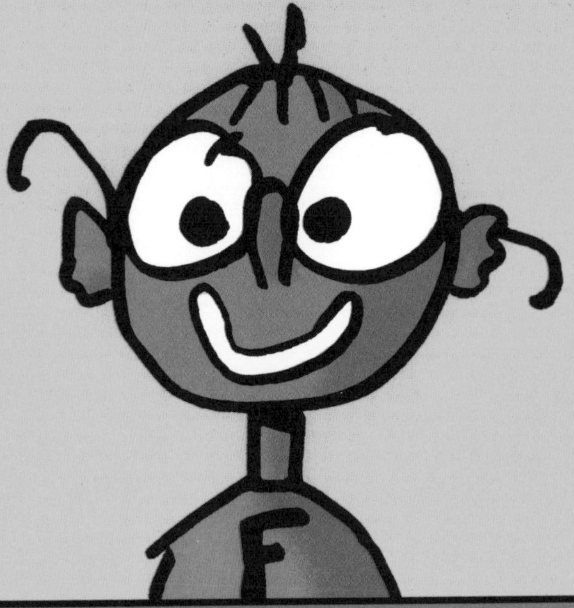
F

Then there's Frank.

Good-guy-Frank, I like to call him. He's a really **super** pal.

He moved to town when he was five. He really gets me. I can tell him stuff and he just understands exactly what I mean.

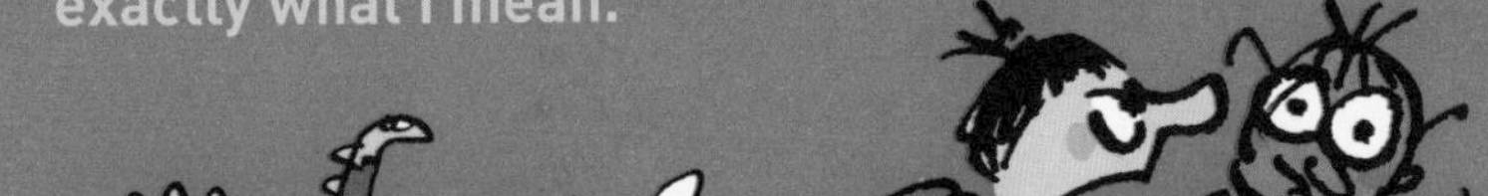

If only we could have lived a thousand years ago, Frank.

You're right, Toby! Just think how much less we'd have to learn in history class!

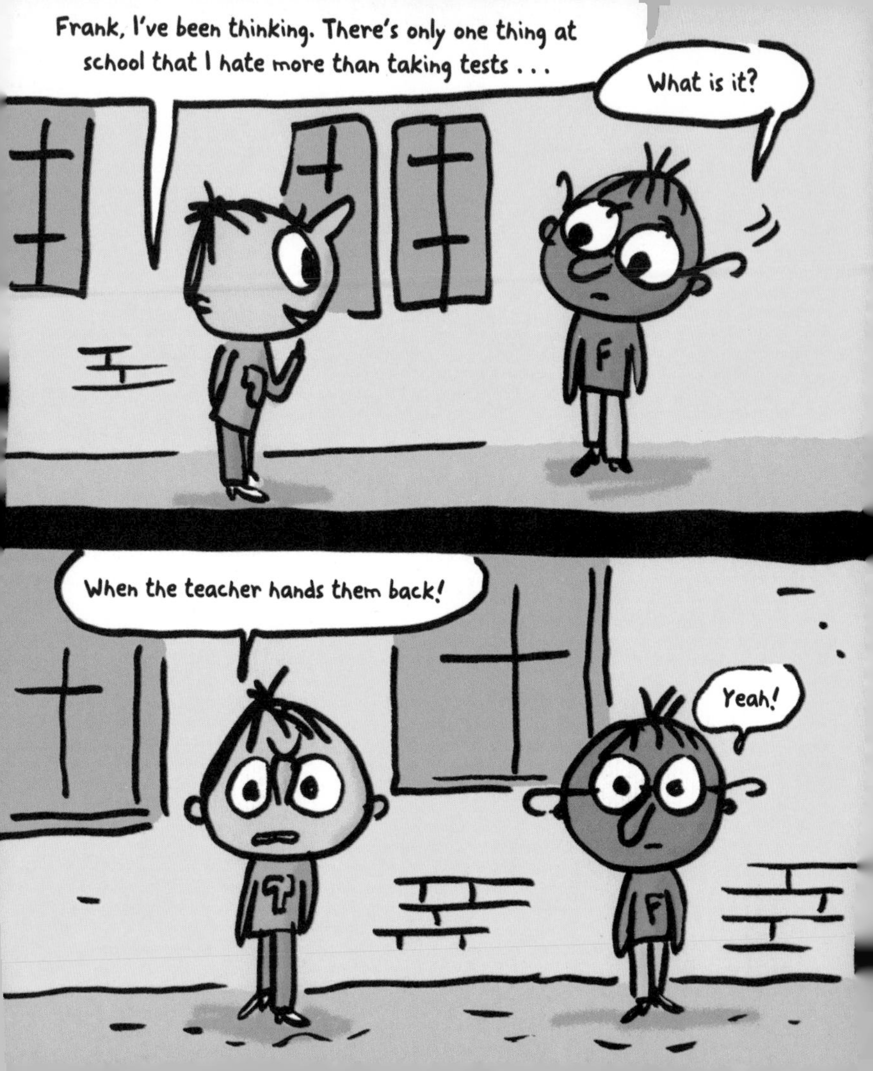
Frank, I've been thinking. There's only one thing at school that I hate more than taking tests . . .
What is it?
When the teacher hands them back!
Yeah!

Well, I guess he doesn't always understand exactly what I mean. . . .

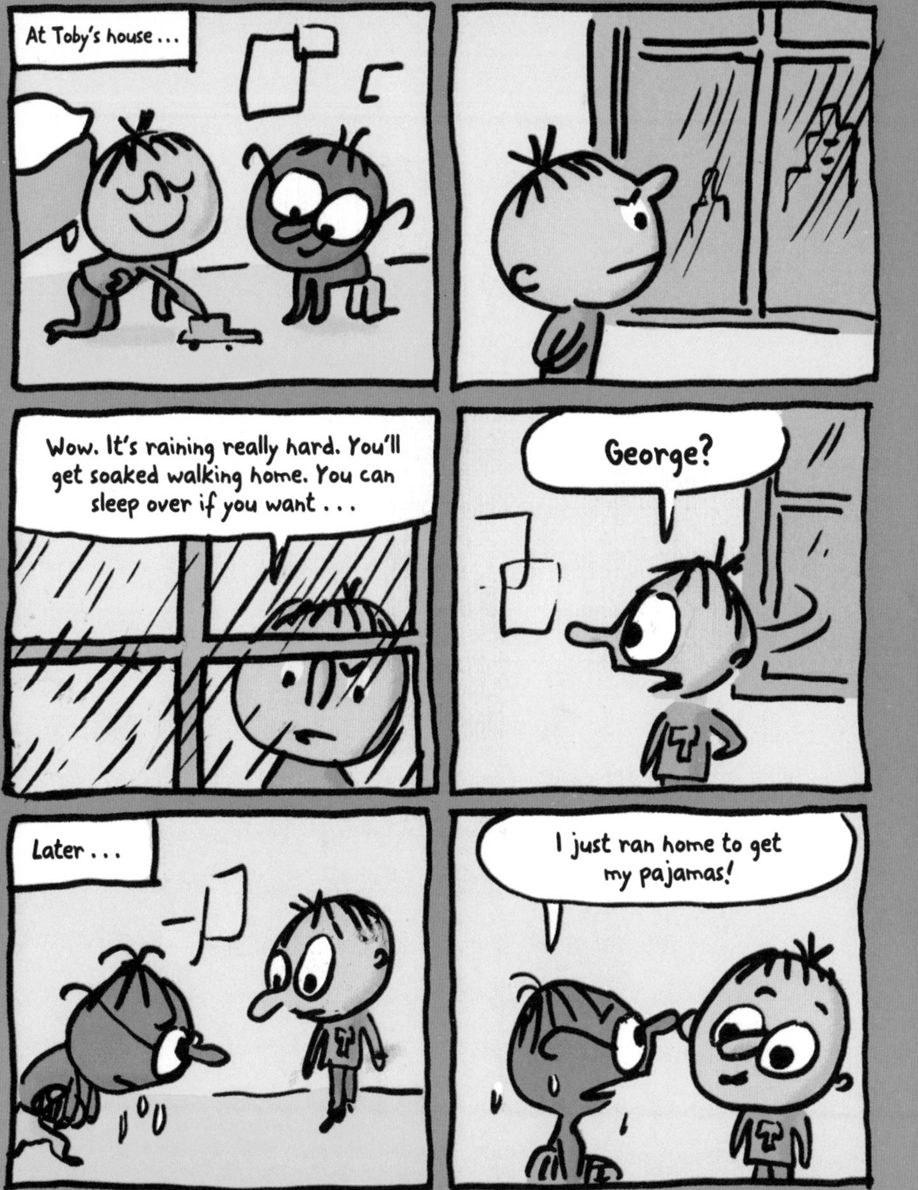
At Toby's house . . .
Wow. It's raining really hard. You'll get soaked walking home. You can sleep over if you want . . .
George?
Later . . .
I just ran home to get my pajamas!

George and Frank are my two main pals, but I have other friends, too.

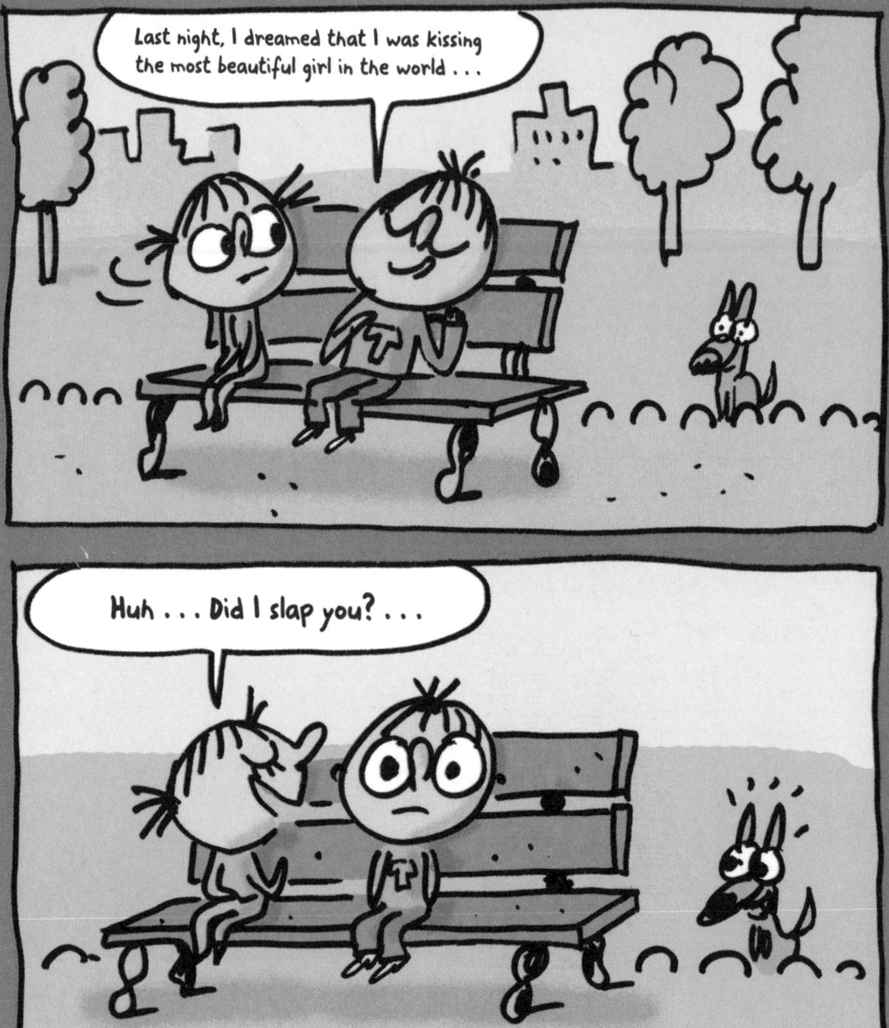
Last night, I dreamed that I was kissing the most beautiful girl in the world . . .
Huh . . . Did I slap you? . . .

Hi, Toby, I saw your friend George the other day, but he didn't see me.

I know, he told me!

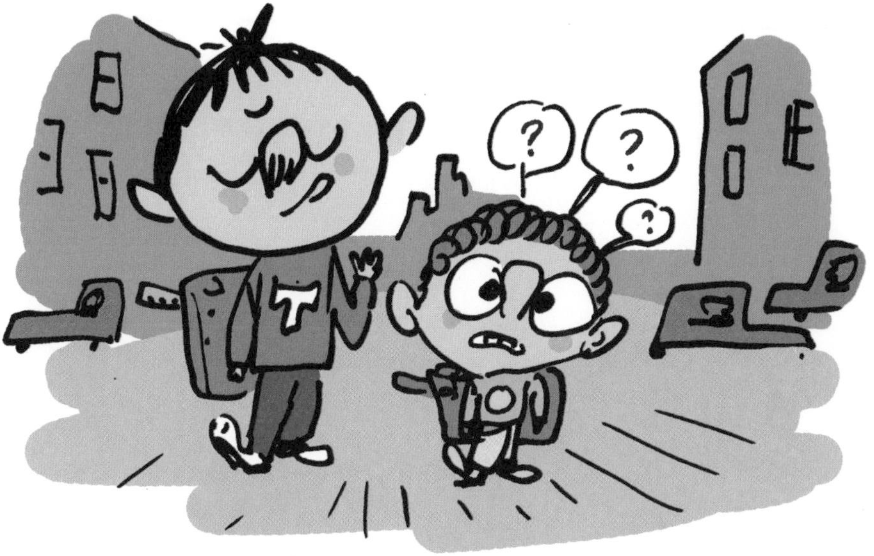
?
?
?

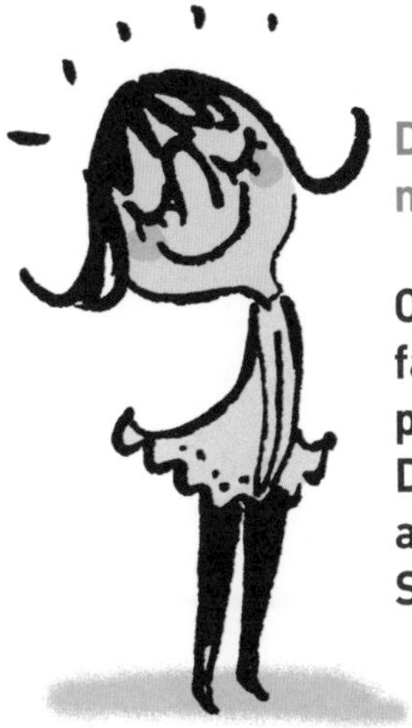

Do you think we'll get married one day?

Oh, I doubt it! In my family we all marry people we're related to: Dad and Mom, Grandpa and Grandma, Aunt Sally and Uncle Rich . . .

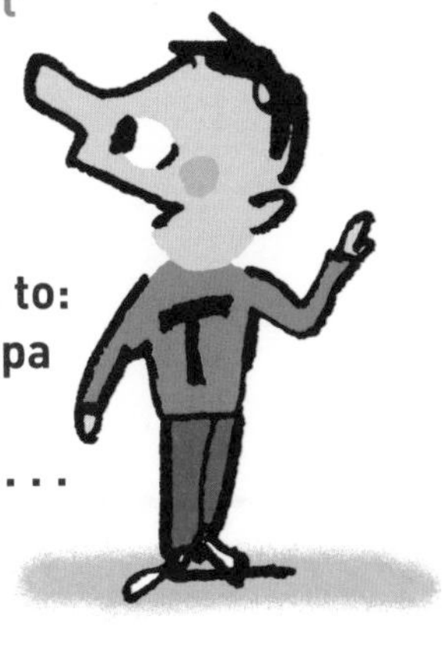

TIME TO TALK ABOUT SCHOOL!!! YAY!!!

I used lots of exclamation points so you think I'm super excited. (That's a lie.)
Or that I have fun in class. (Another lie.)

My teacher once said that a person will spend one third of their life sleeping. I'm almost nine, so that means I've been asleep for three whole years already!

If you add all the time I've been in school to the time I've been sleeping, **I'VE HAD NO LIFE AT ALL!**

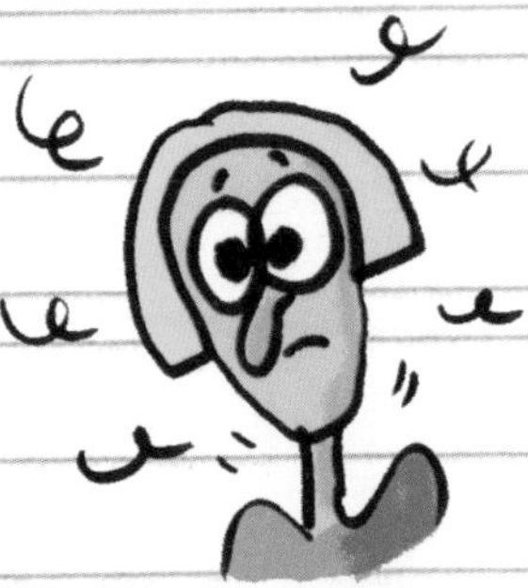

Good morning, children, I'm your new teacher. Does anyone know what my name is?

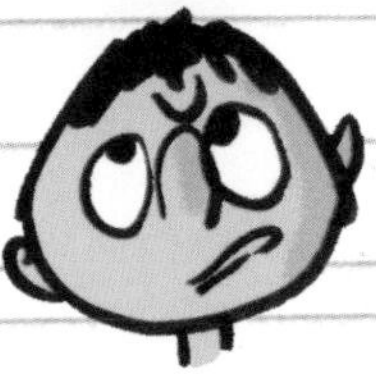

Oh, man! It's only the first day of school and you're already asking trick questions . . .

It's Mrs. SMITH, Toby!

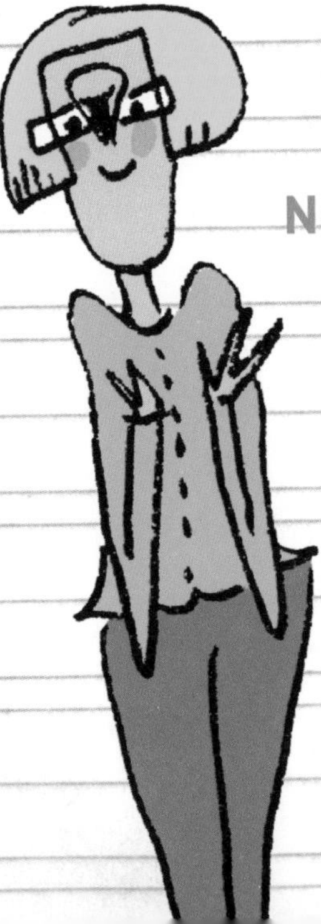

If I say, "I was pretty," that's past tense.

Now, if I say, "I'm pretty," what's that, Toby?

A lie?

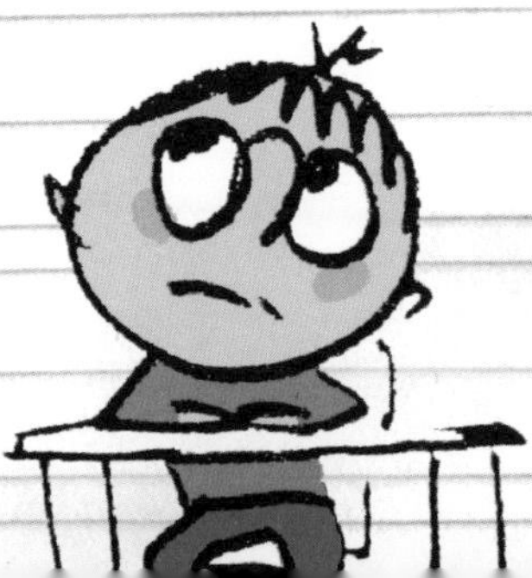

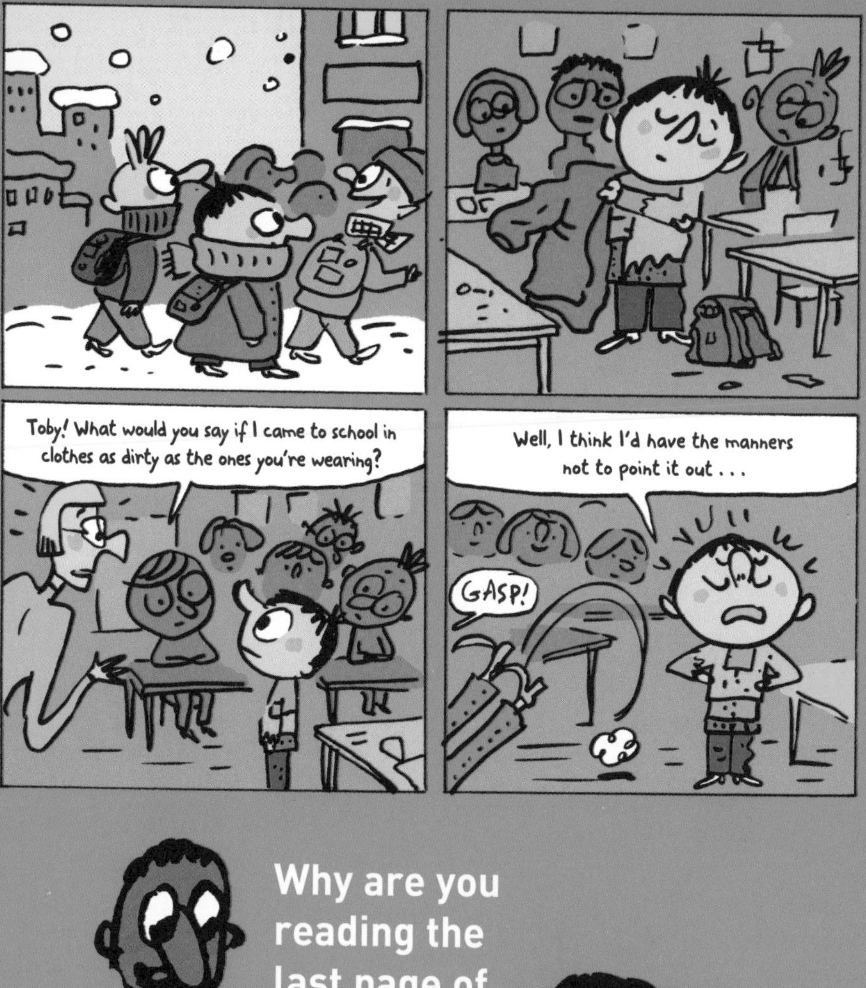
Toby! What would you say if I came to school in clothes as dirty as the ones you're wearing?
Well, I think I'd have the manners not to point it out . . .
GASP!

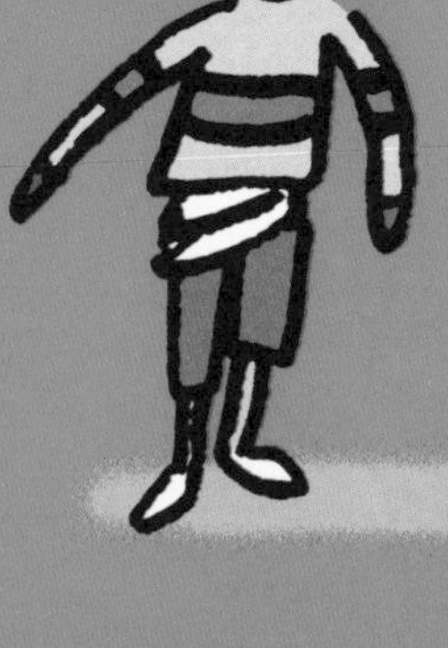

Why are you reading the last page of the history textbook?

I want to know how it ends!

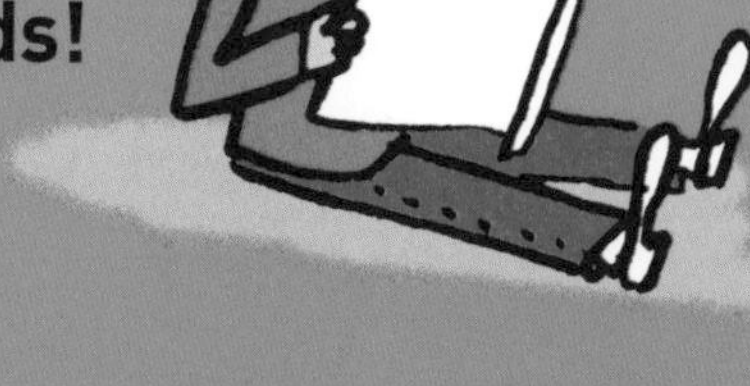

Toby, name a day of the week that starts with the letter "T."

TOMORROW!

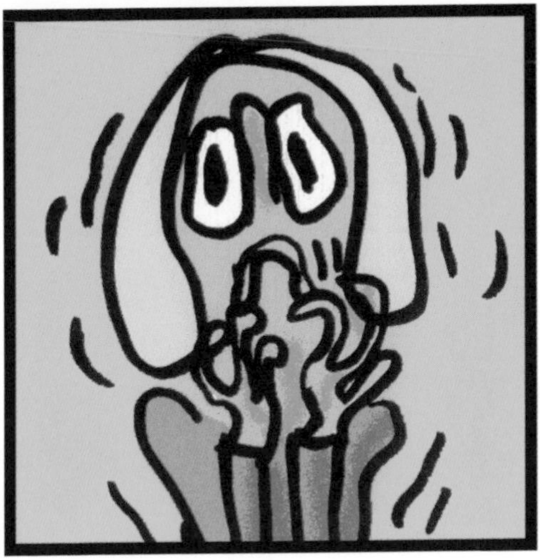

Mrs. Smith, I reread my paper, and I don't think I should have received a zero.

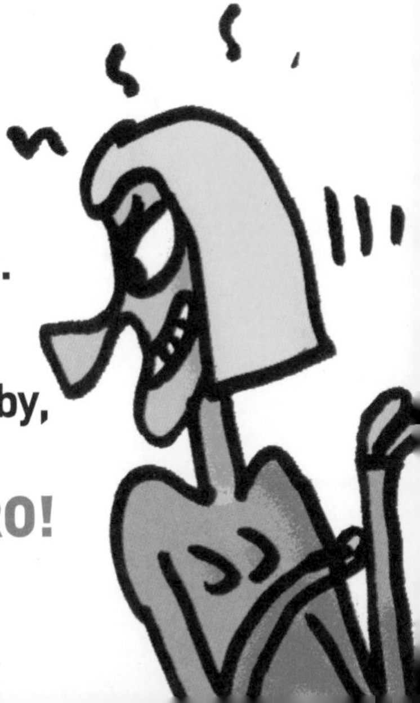

I agree with you, Toby, but I can't give you **LESS THAN ZERO!**

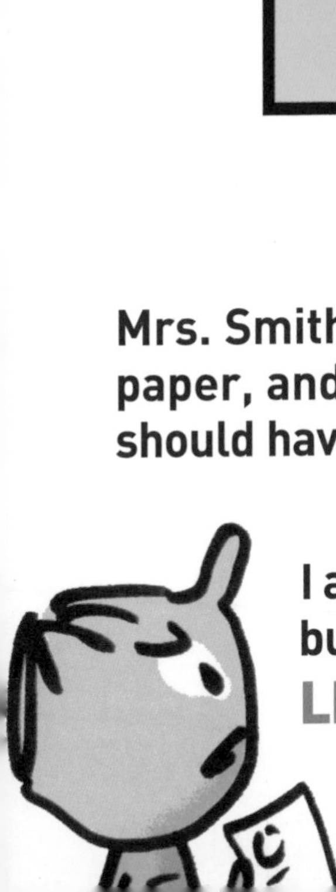

Sometimes I think the teachers don't have to drive very far to get to

CRAZYTOWN.

I don't even have to go out of my way to get under their skin. All I have to be is myself!

Toby, I asked you to copy this sentence ten times to practice your terrible handwriting . . . and you only did it nine times! Why?

I'm bad at math, too.

Toby, how many planets are in the universe?

ALL OF THEM!

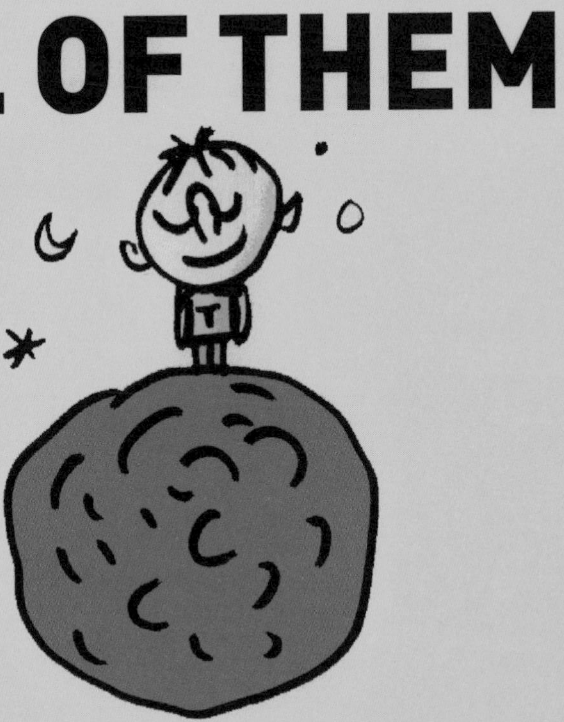

Toby, if you add 4,578 and 6,246, then divide the result by 4 and then multiply by 8, what do you get?

The wrong answer, if you're asking me!

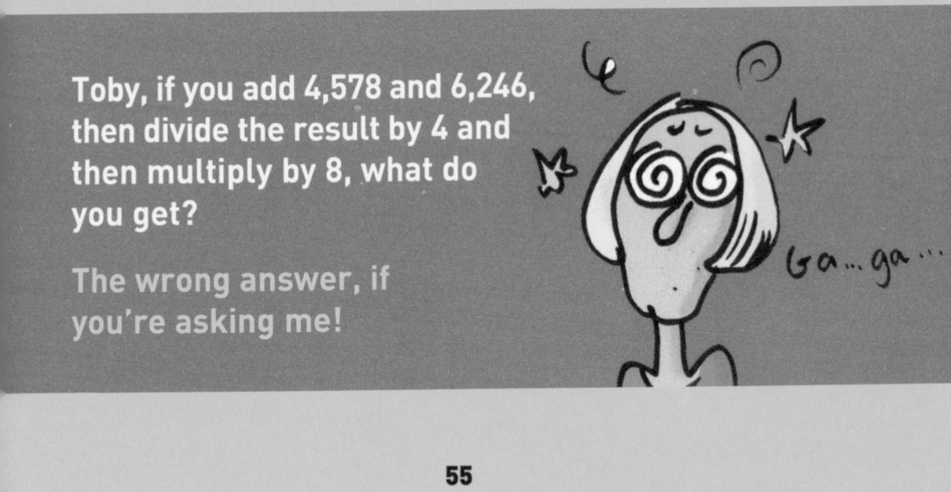
Ga... ga...

TOBY, WHAT ARE YOU DOING STANDING ON A CHAIR?!

Well . . . you told me to sing it higher!

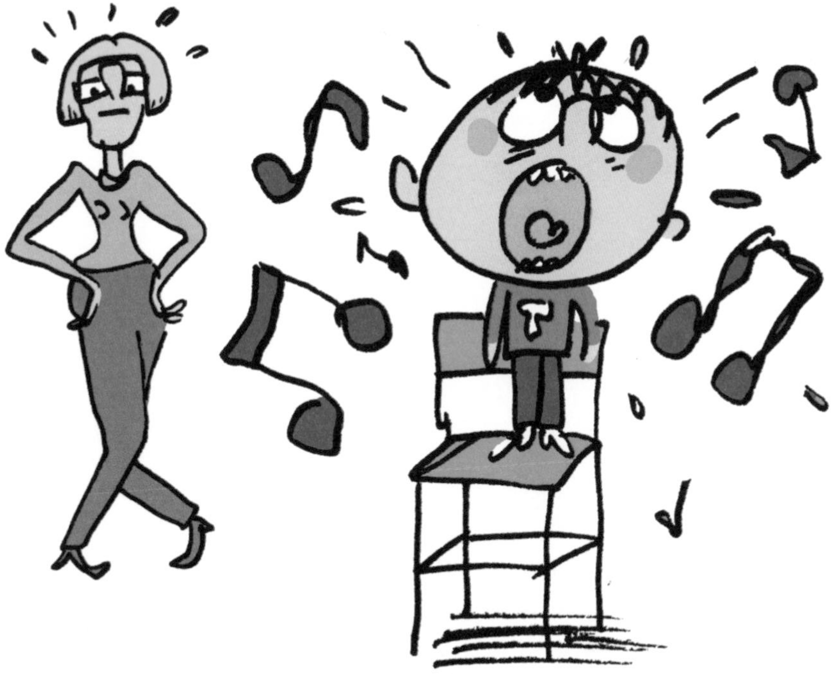

T

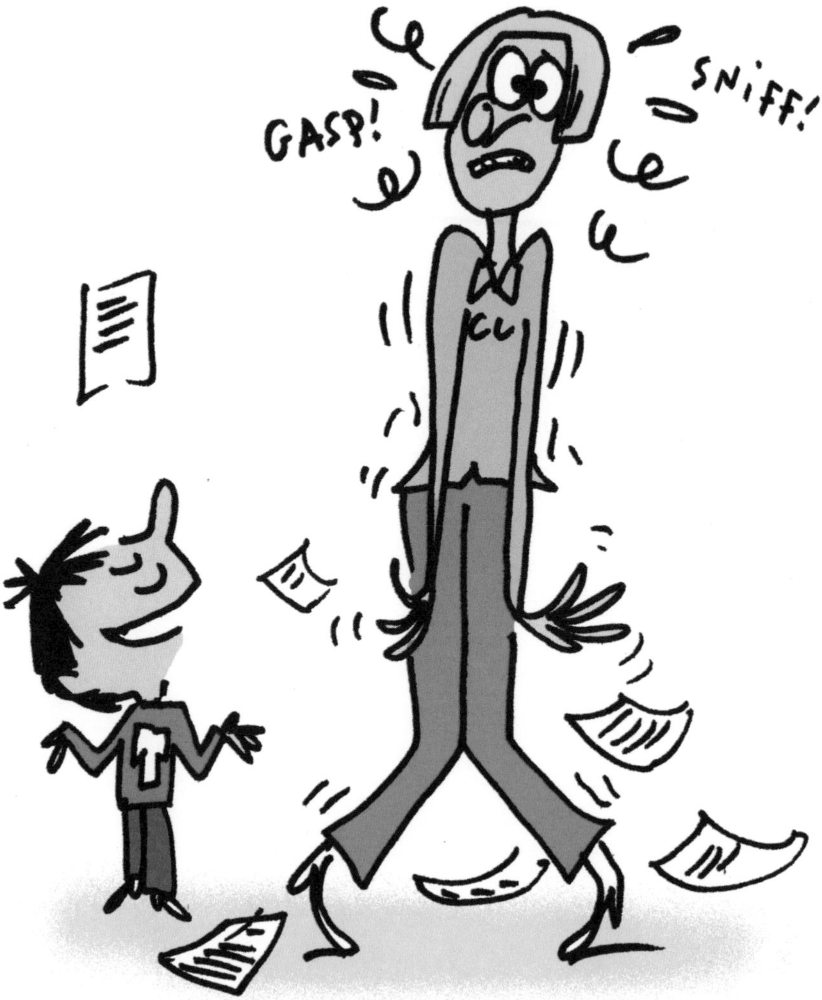
GASP!
SNIFF!

Toby, give me three reasons you know that the Earth is round, not flat.

First, my dad told me it is round. Next, my mom told me, too. Now you just told me. So it MUST be true!

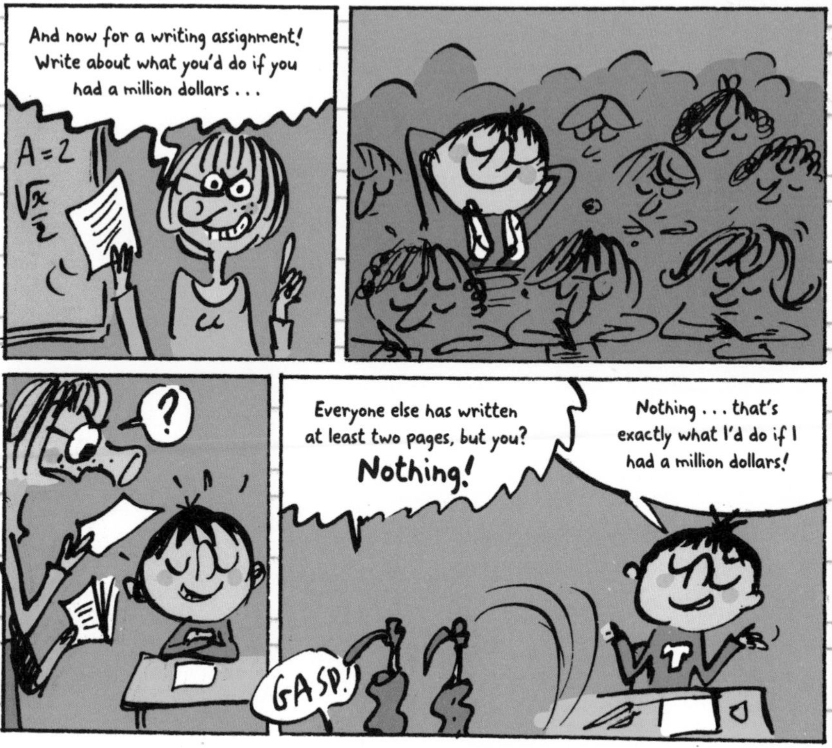
And now for a writing assignment! Write about what you'd do if you had a million dollars . . .
A = 2
?
Everyone else has written at least two pages, but you? Nothing!
Nothing . . . that's exactly what I'd do if I had a million dollars!
GASP!

Mrs. Smith, I'm sorry, but I just can't figure out this problem.

But Toby, a five-year-old would be able to do this!!

Oh, NOW I understand why I can't do it! I'm going to be nine soon!

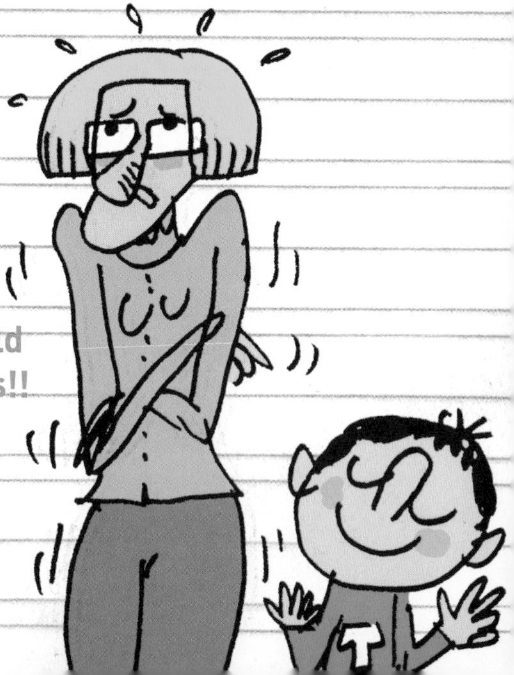

Toby, this is the first time you've handed in your homework since the beginning of the year! Why??

I just didn't have enough time to make up an excuse!

Toby, what did you do this weekend?

I talked to a Martian!

Really now, Toby.
Martians live on Mars . . .

Well, yeah, I had to
yell really loud!

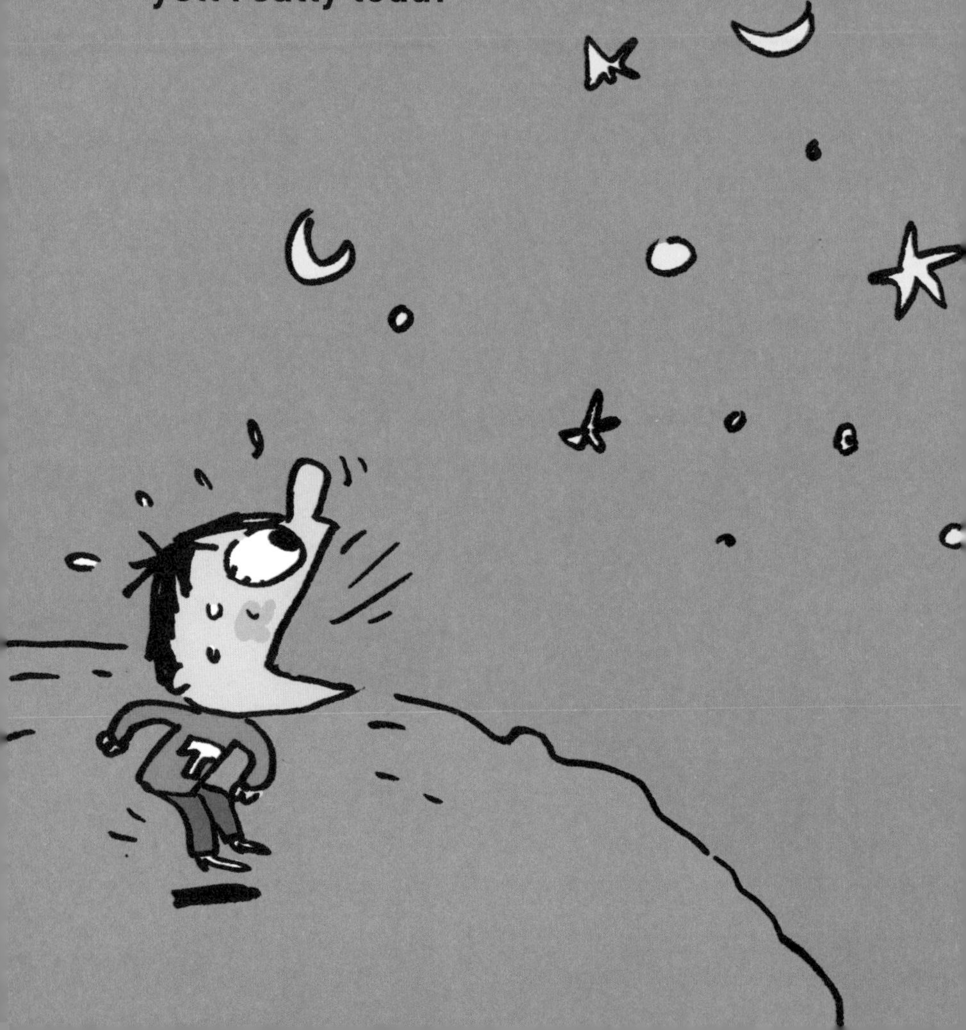

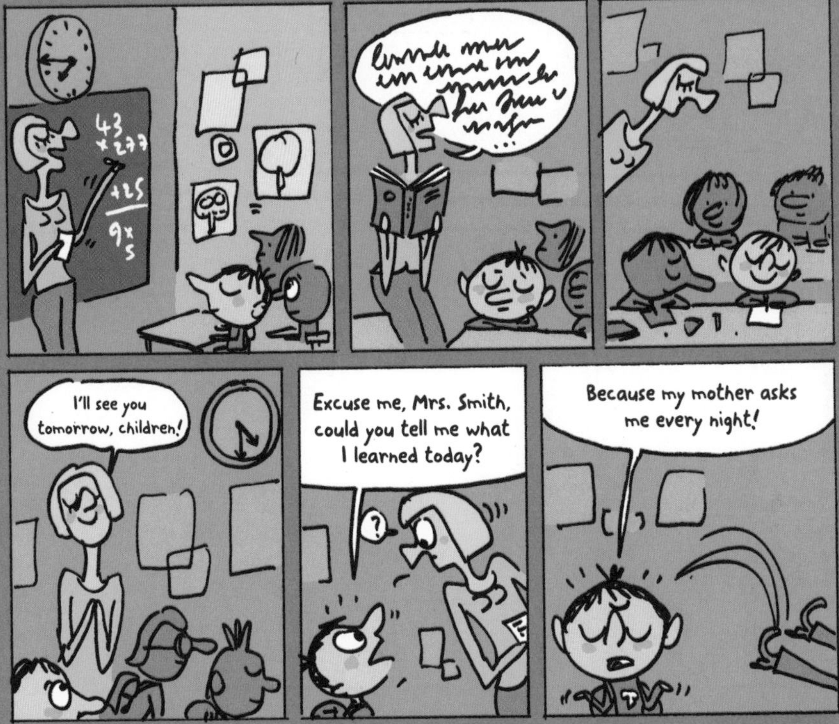
I'll see you tomorrow, children!
Excuse me, Mrs. Smith, could you tell me what I learned today?
Because my mother asks me every night!

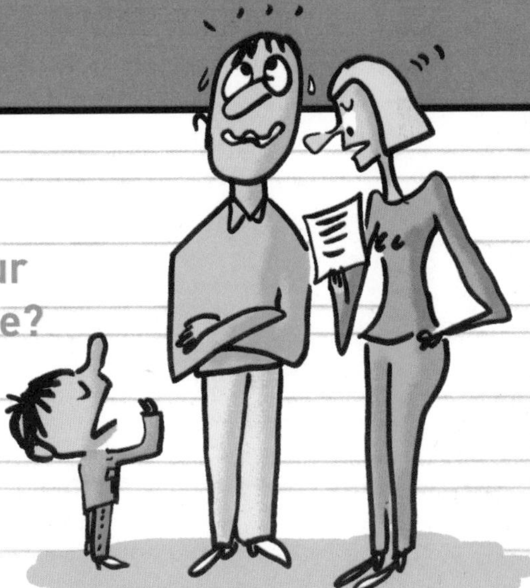

Toby, your father helped you with your homework, didn't he?

NO! Mrs. Smith, I swear! He did it all by himself . . .

But school isn't all work and no play. After all, it's where my friends are five days a week!

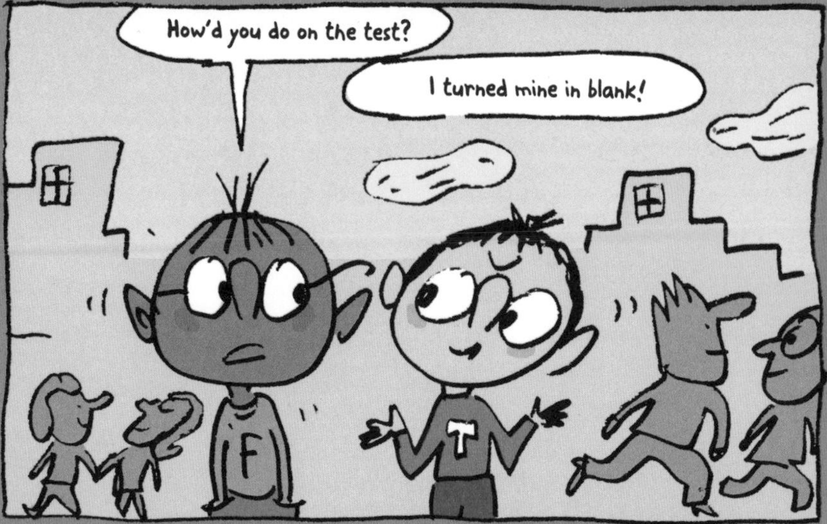
How'd you do on the test?
I turned mine in blank!
F
T

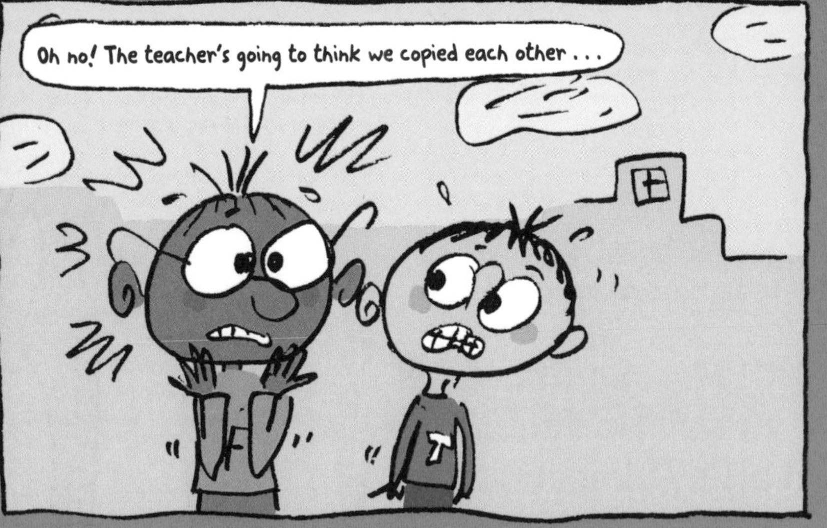
Oh no! The teacher's going to think we copied each other . . .
T

GOOD NEWS!

The teacher said we had a test today, rain or shine!

So what's the good news?

It's SNOWING!

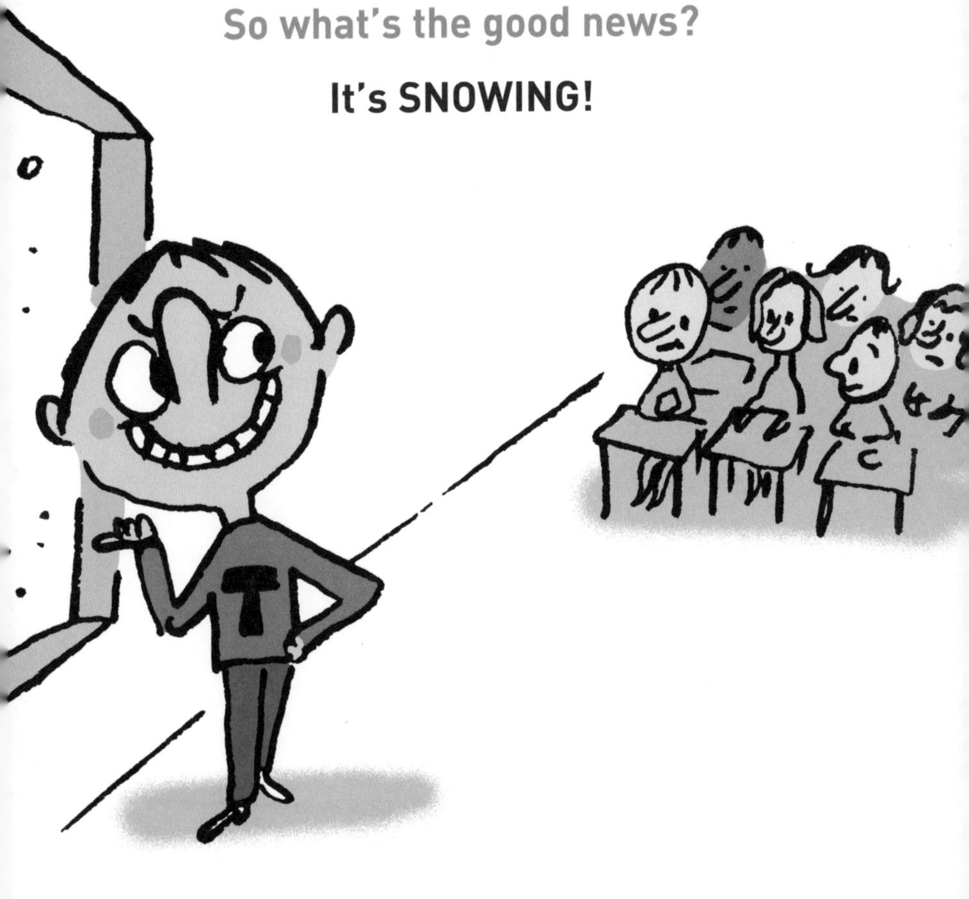

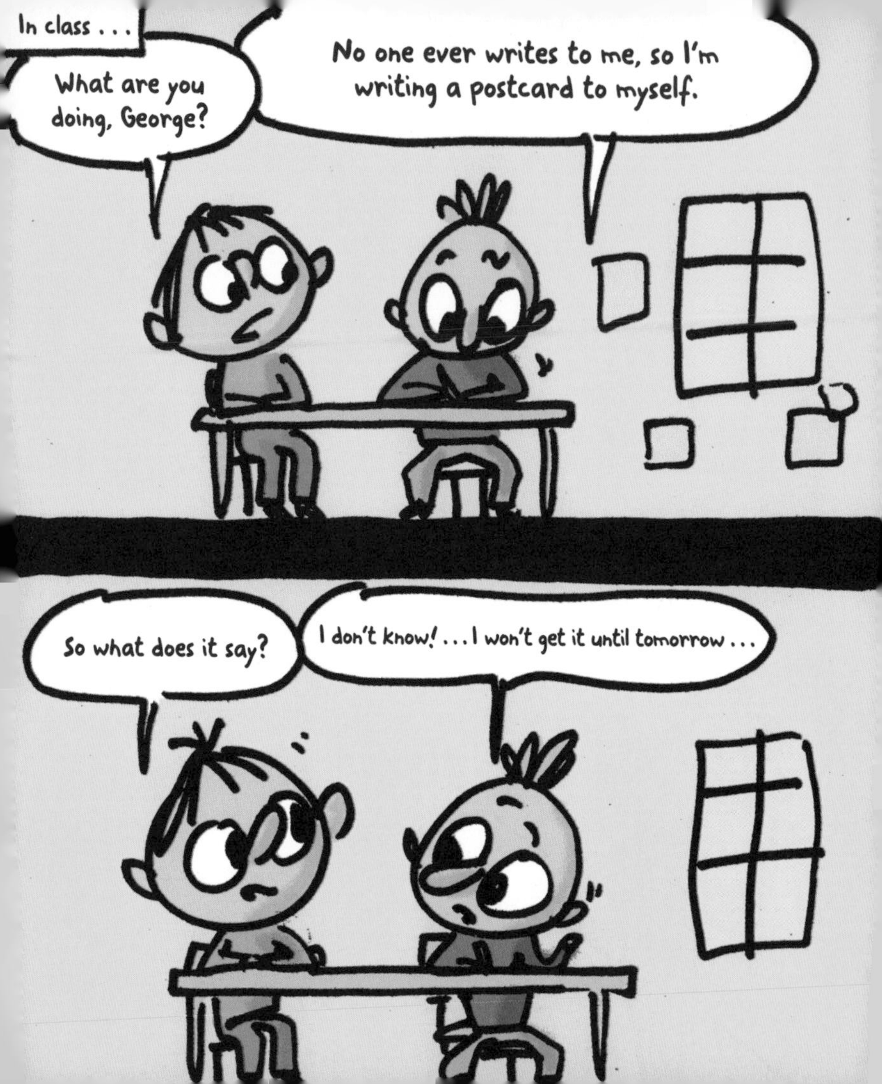
In class . . .
What are you doing, George?
No one ever writes to me, so I'm writing a postcard to myself.
So what does it say?
I don't know! . . . I won't get it until tomorrow . . .

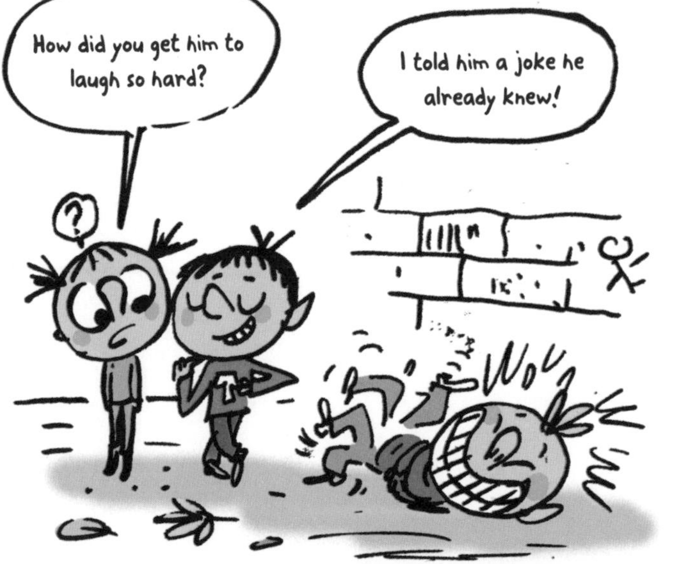
How did you get him to laugh so hard?
I told him a joke he already knew!

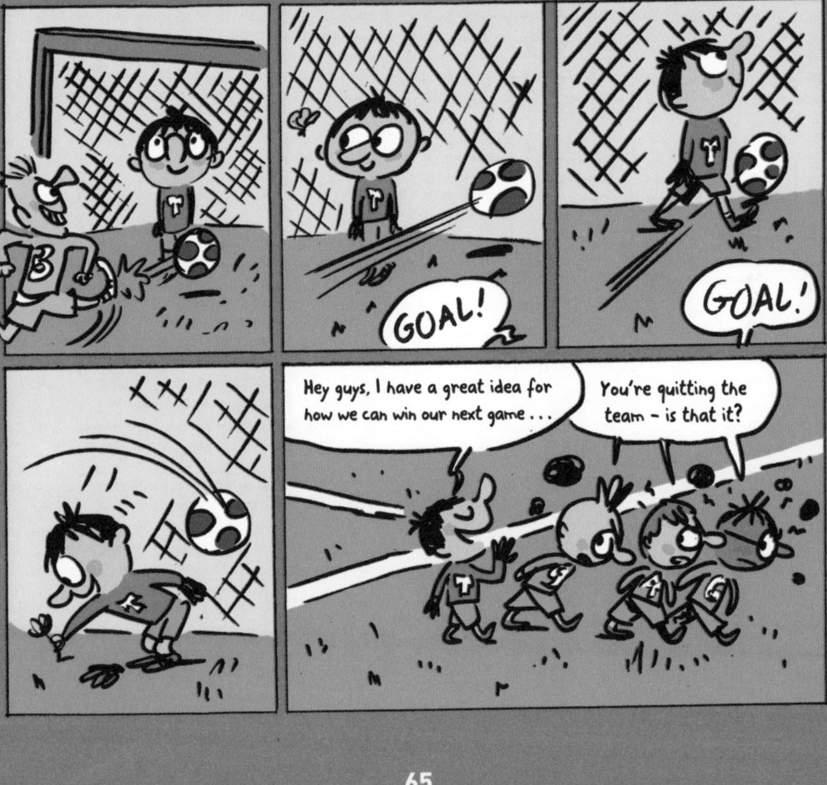
GOAL!
GOAL!
Hey guys, I have a great idea for how we can win our next game . . .
You're quitting the team – is that it?

Then again, I'm not ALWAYS on my best behavior. Sometimes I just have to let loose and go a little nuts. Even if it gets me in trouble!

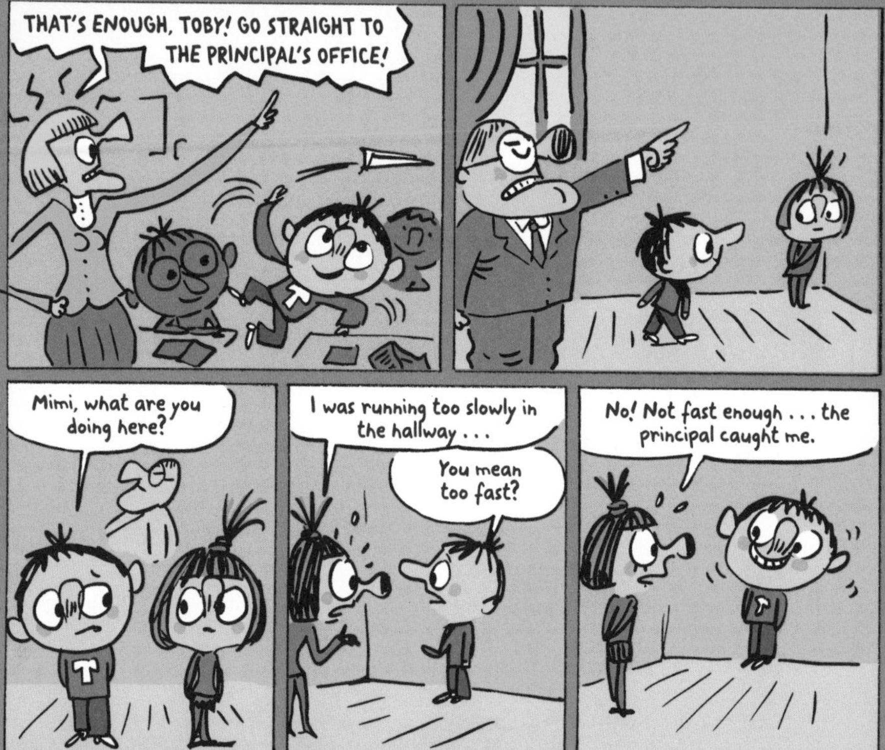

THAT'S ENOUGH, TOBY! GO STRAIGHT TO THE PRINCIPAL'S OFFICE!
Mimi, what are you doing here?
I was running too slowly in the hallway . . .
You mean too fast?
No! Not fast enough . . . the principal caught me.

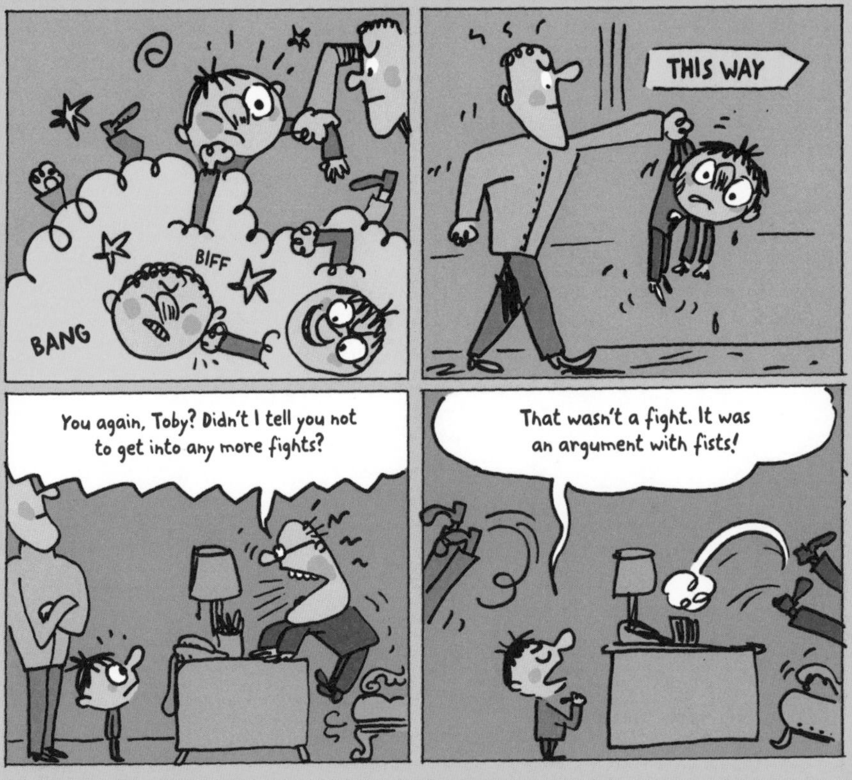
BIFF
BANG
THIS WAY
You again, Toby? Didn't I tell you not to get into any more fights?
That wasn't a fight. It was an argument with fists!

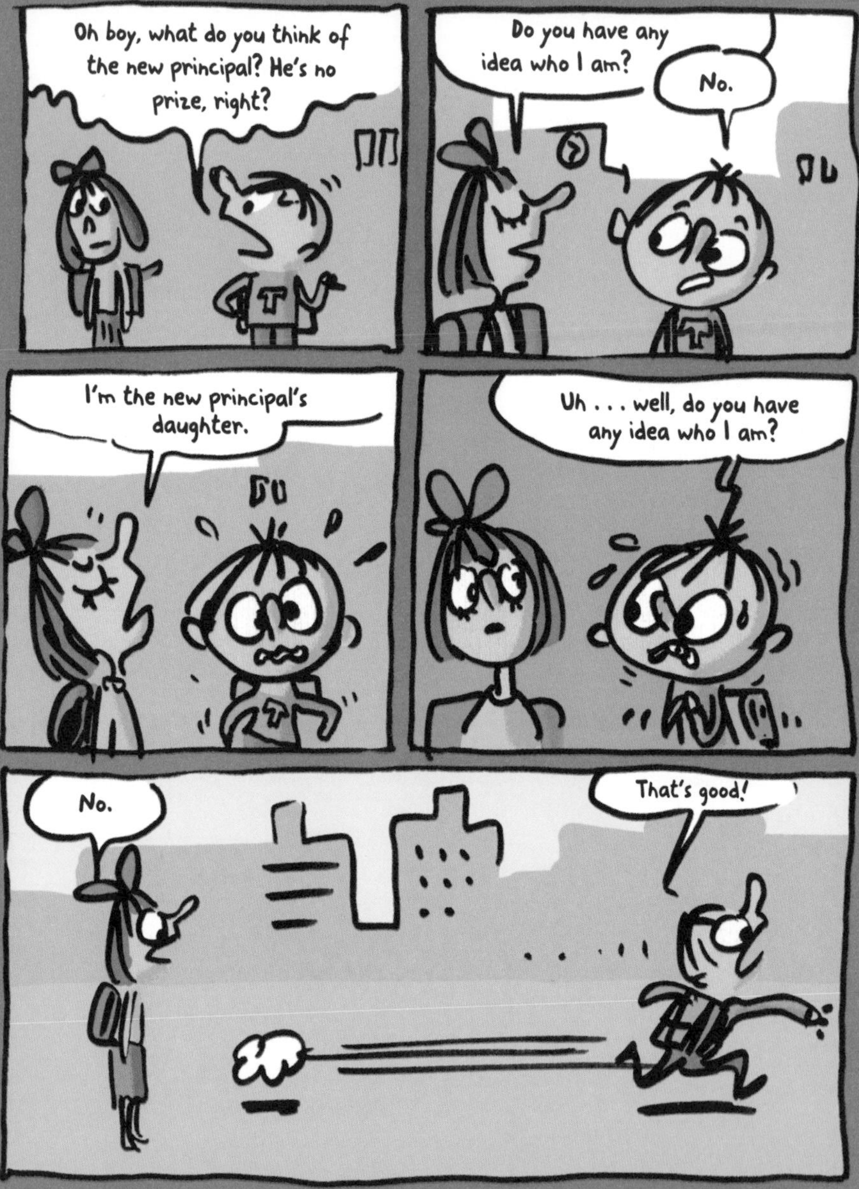
Oh boy, what do you think of the new principal? He's no prize, right?
Do you have any idea who I am?
No.
I'm the new principal's daughter.
Uh . . . well, do you have any idea who I am?
No.
That's good!

One of my favorite ways to let loose is to answer the teacher's questions.

YUP, YOU HEARD ME!

But don't get me wrong. When I give an answer, it's almost **NEVER** the answer they want to hear! They never laugh, but that's what I think is hilarious.

(Maybe I'll be a comedian someday!)

Toby, I asked you to solve the word problem about the leaky faucet. Your answer is completely **WRONG!** How did you come up with 555-978-4432 for an answer?

It's the plumber's phone number,

DUH!

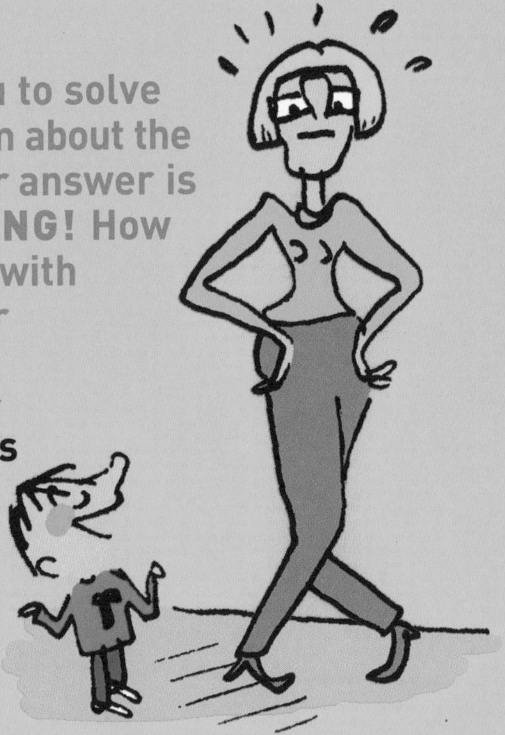

Toby, we don't play
games while we work!

But I'm **NOT WORKING**, Mrs. Smith!

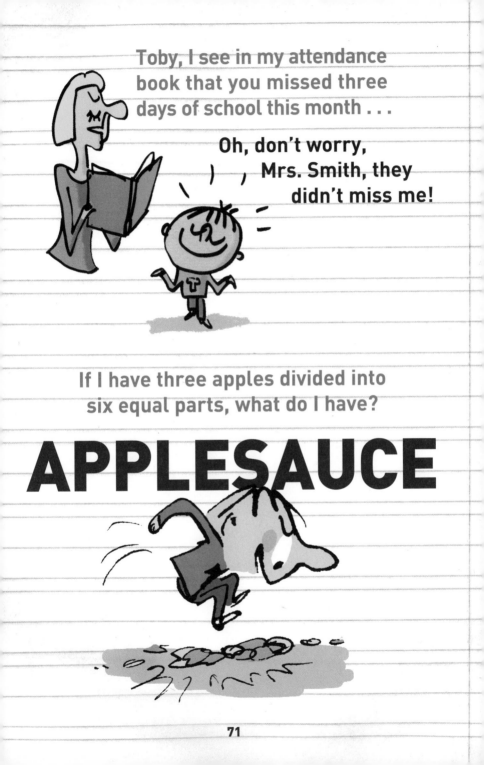

Toby, I see in my attendance book that you missed three days of school this month . . .

Oh, don't worry, Mrs. Smith, they didn't miss me!

If I have three apples divided into six equal parts, what do I have?

APPLESAUCE

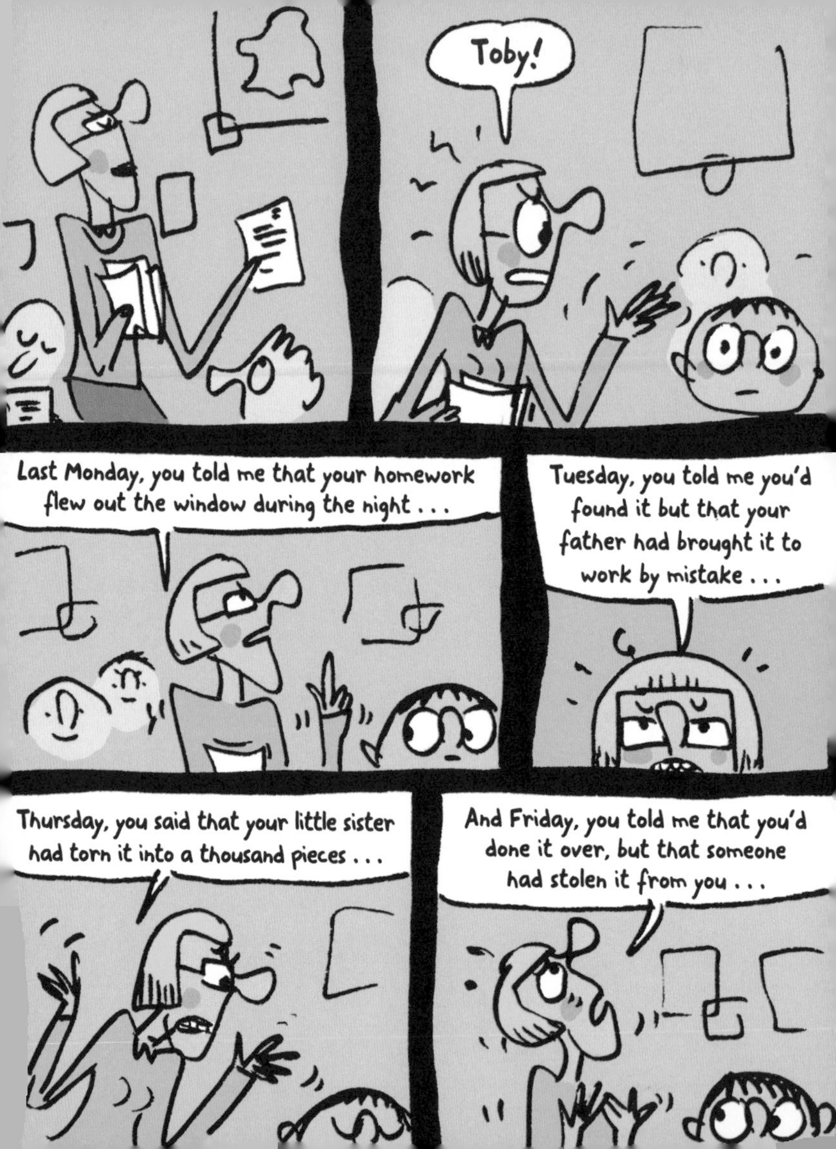
Toby!
Last Monday, you told me that your homework flew out the window during the night . . .
Tuesday, you told me you'd found it but that your father had brought it to work by mistake . . .
Thursday, you said that your little sister had torn it into a thousand pieces . . .
And Friday, you told me that you'd done it over, but that someone had stolen it from you . . .

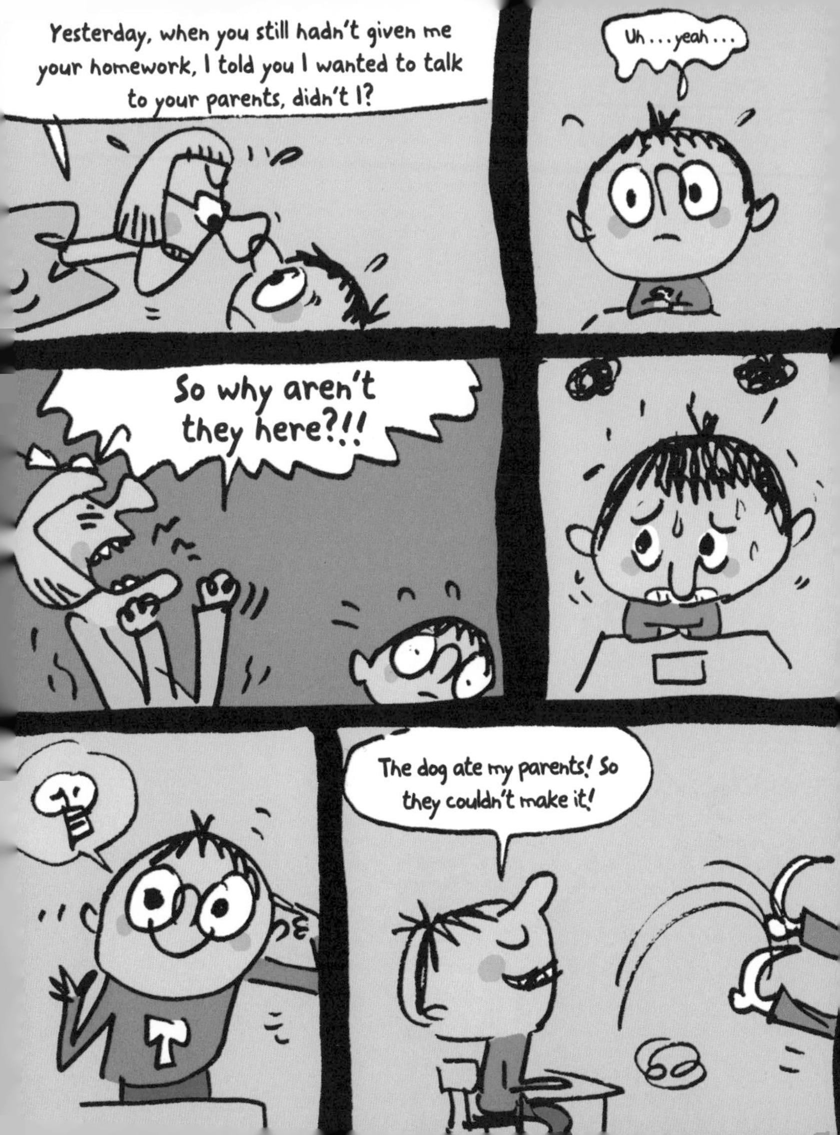

Yesterday, when you still hadn't given me your homework, I told you I wanted to talk to your parents, didn't I?
Uh . . . yeah . . .
So why aren't they here?!!
The dog ate my parents! So they couldn't make it!

How many letters
are there in the alphabet?

8!

What do you mean, **8**?

A...L...P...H...A...B...E...T...
That makes **8**.

For the most part, getting through the school day isn't so hard. I try to have fun, crack some jokes, and talk to my friends. But there are two parts of the day that always bum me out. **LUNCH** and **QUIZZES.**

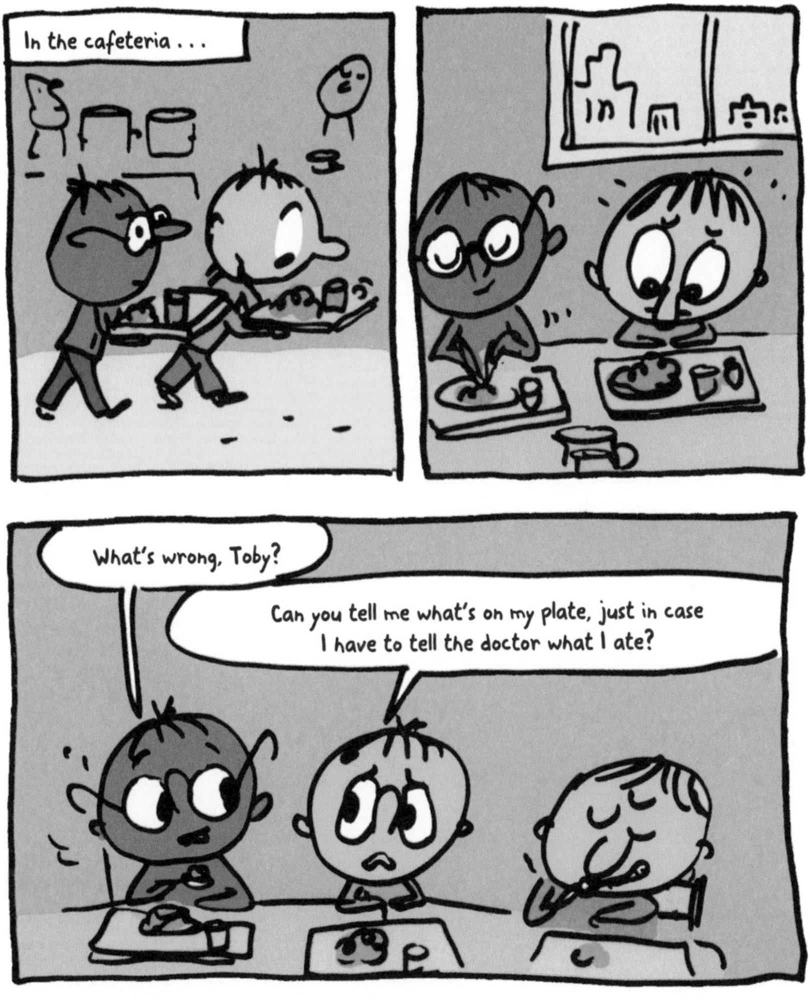
In the cafeteria . . .
What's wrong, Toby?
Can you tell me what's on my plate, just in case I have to tell the doctor what I ate?

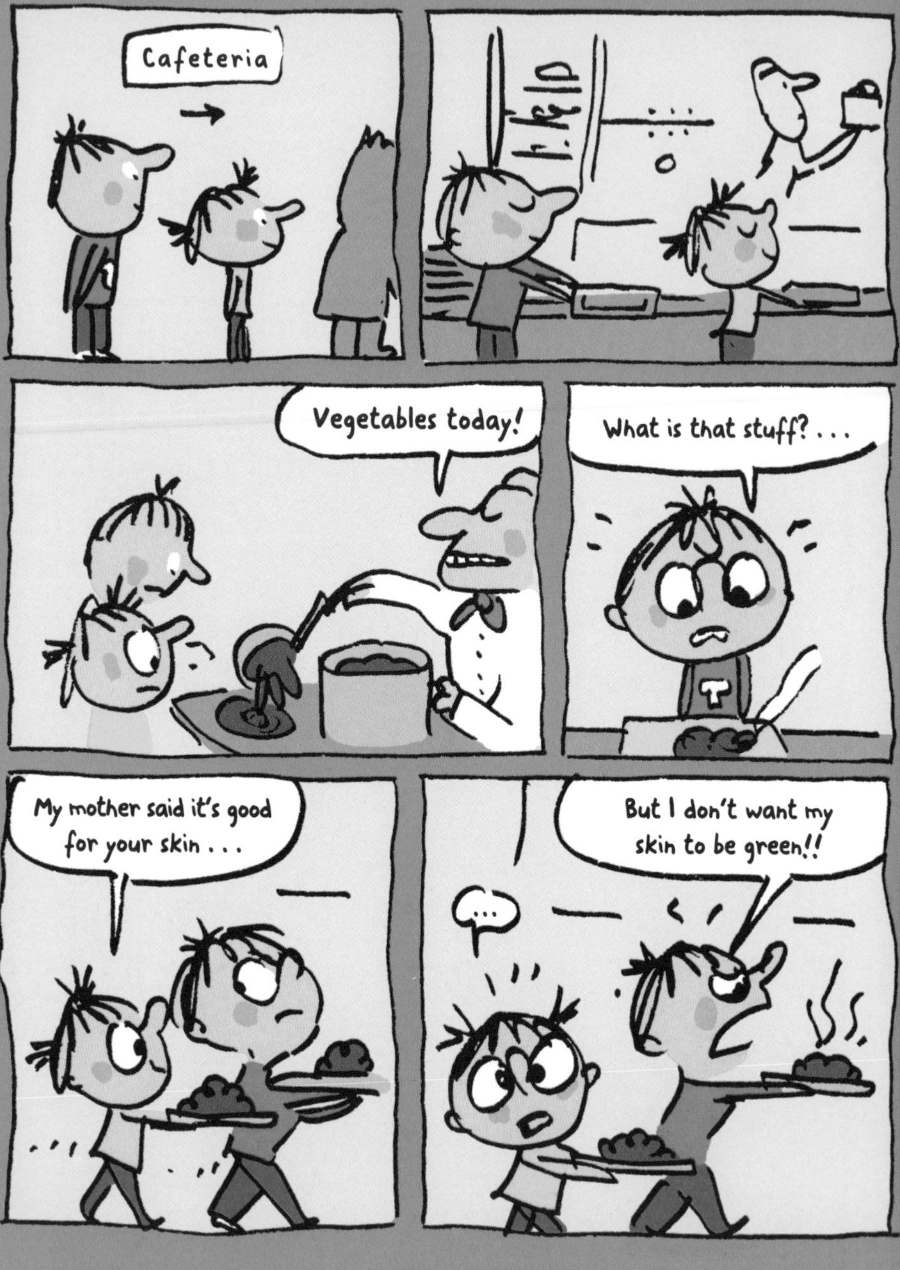
Cafeteria
Vegetables today!
What is that stuff? . . .
My mother said it's good for your skin . . .
...
But I don't want my skin to be green!!

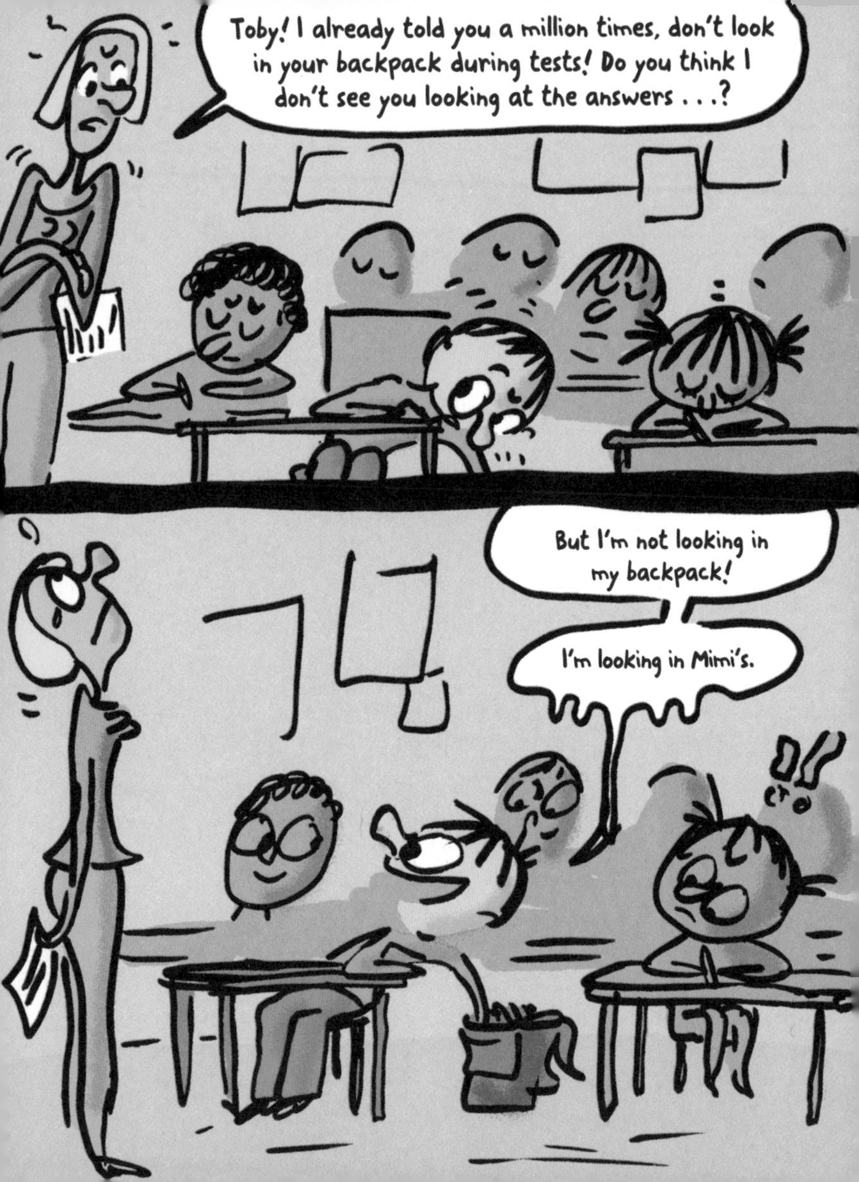
Toby! I already told you a million times, don't look in your backpack during tests! Do you think I don't see you looking at the answers . . .?
But I'm not looking in my backpack!
I'm looking in Mimi's.

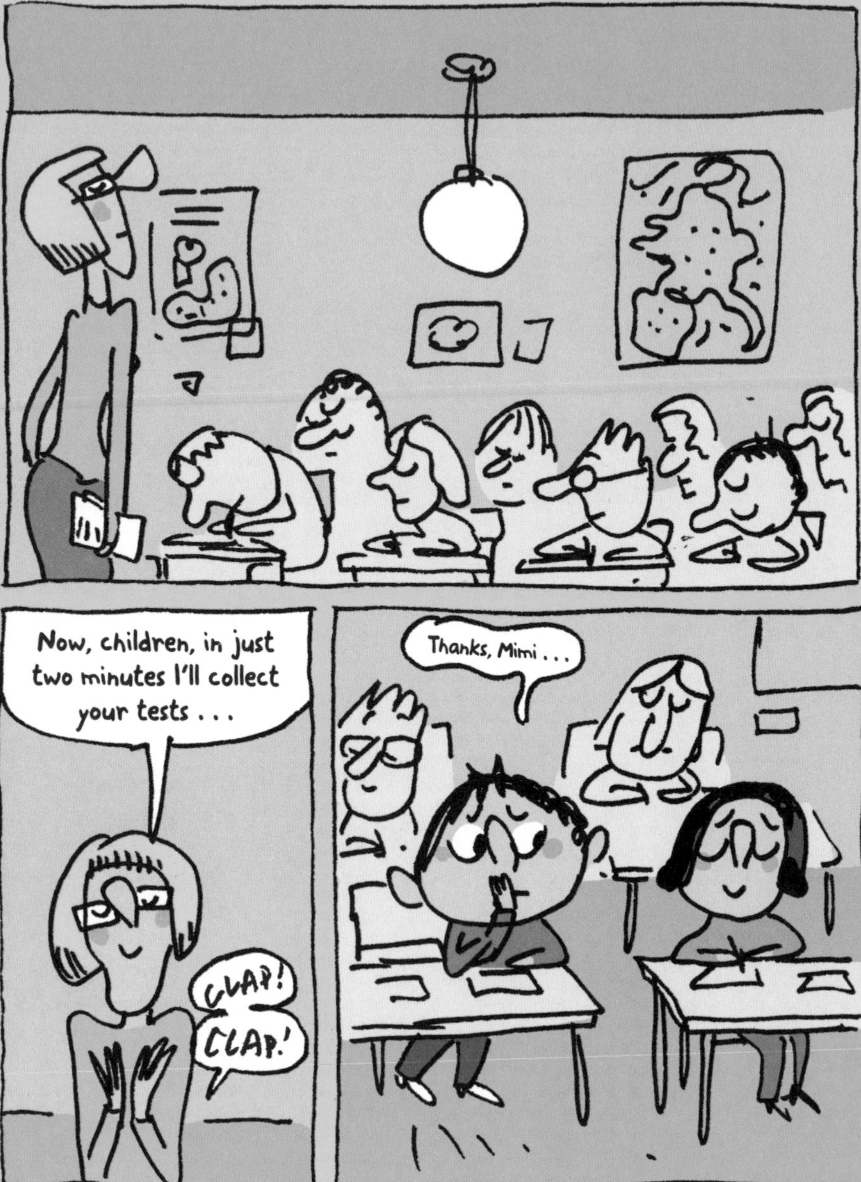
Now, children, in just two minutes I'll collect your tests . . .
CLAP!
CLAP!
Thanks, Mimi . . .

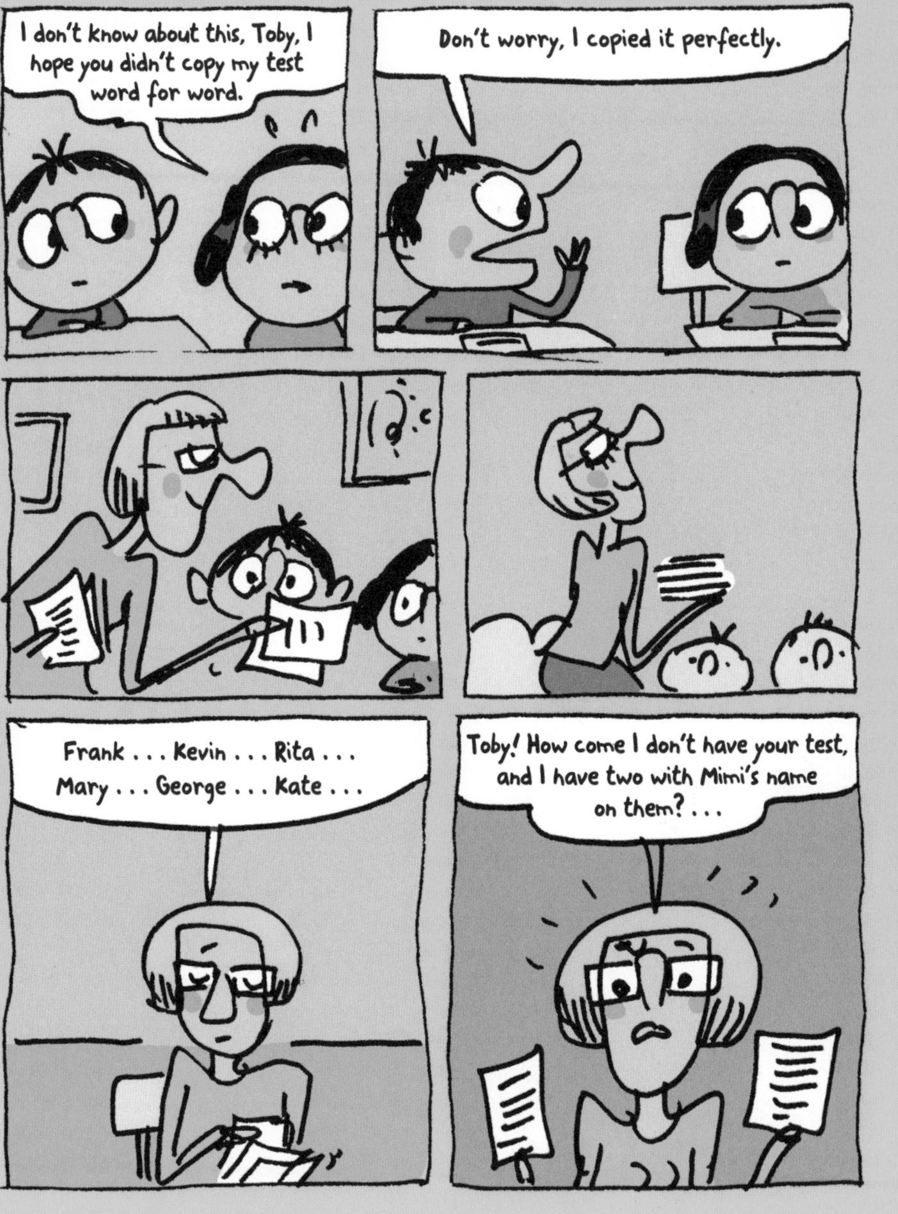
I don't know about this, Toby, I hope you didn't copy my test word for word.
Don't worry, I copied it perfectly.
Frank . . . Kevin . . . Rita . . . Mary . . . George . . . Kate . . .
Toby! How come I don't have your test, and I have two with Mimi's name on them? . . .

Of course, the worst part of any day is coming home with a bad report card or a note from my teacher about getting in trouble.

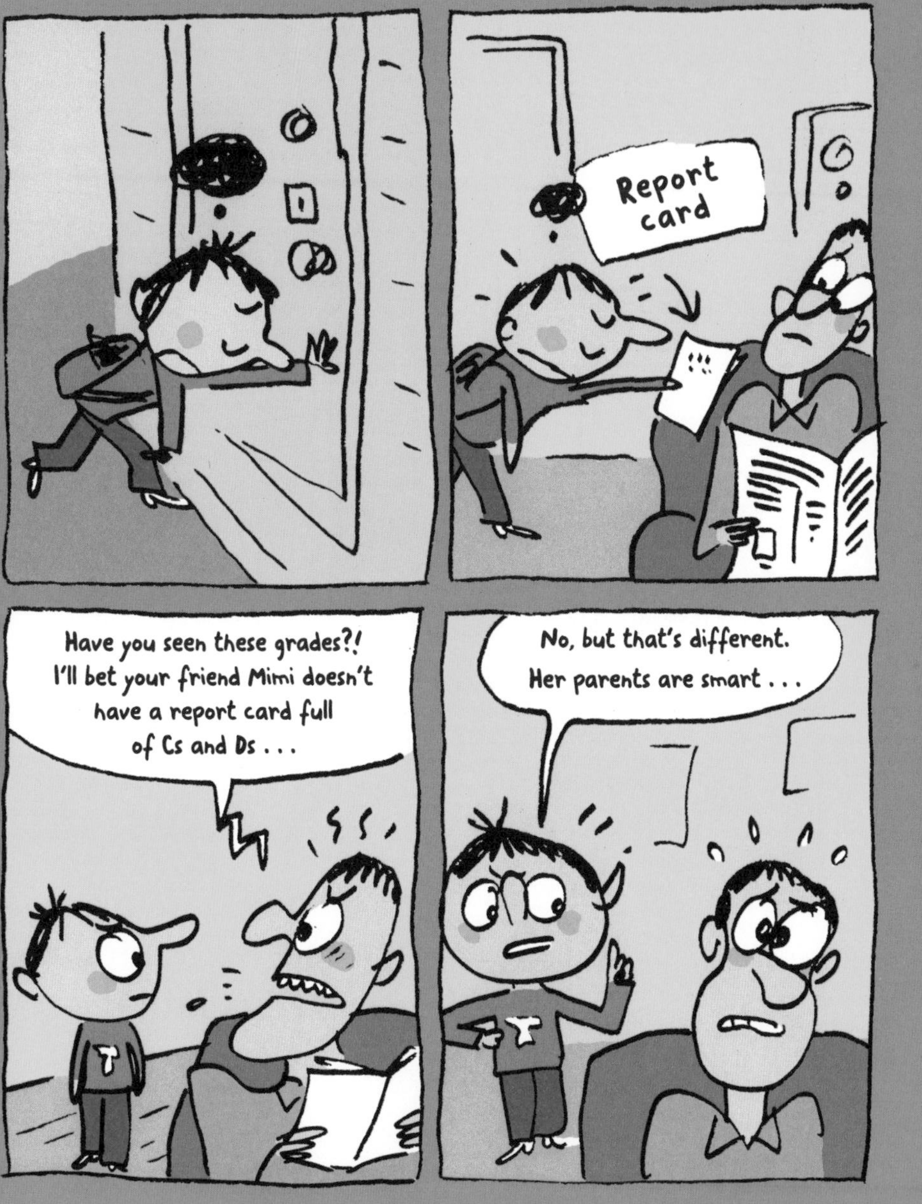
Report card
Have you seen these grades?! I'll bet your friend Mimi doesn't have a report card full of Cs and Ds . . .
No, but that's different. Her parents are smart . . .

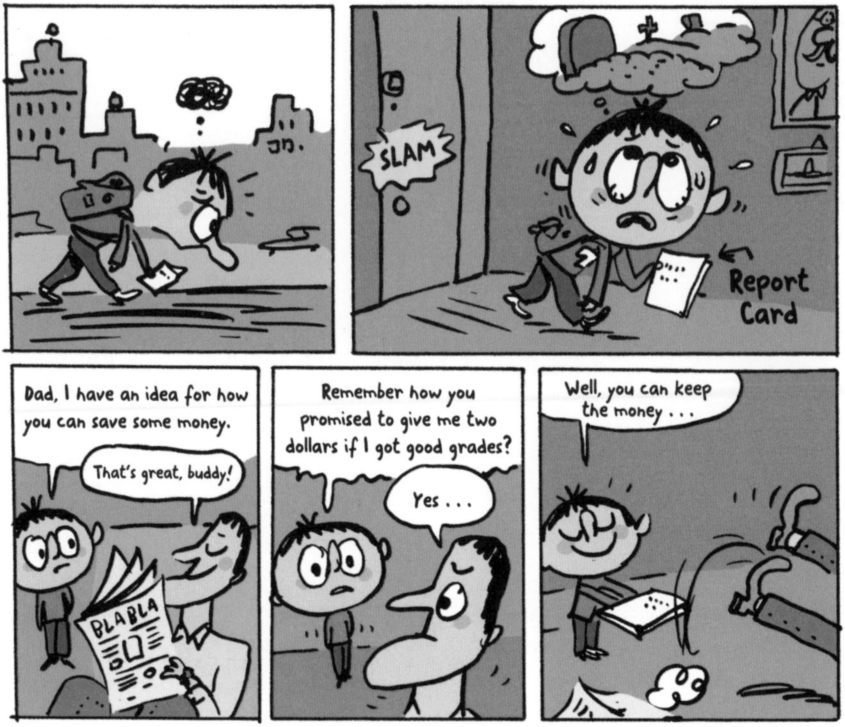

SLAM
Report Card
Dad, I have an idea for how you can save some money.
That's great, buddy!
BLABLA
Remember how you promised to give me two dollars if I got good grades?
Yes . . .
Well, you can keep the money . . .

Toby, where's your report card?

I loaned it to my friend. He wanted to scare his father . . .

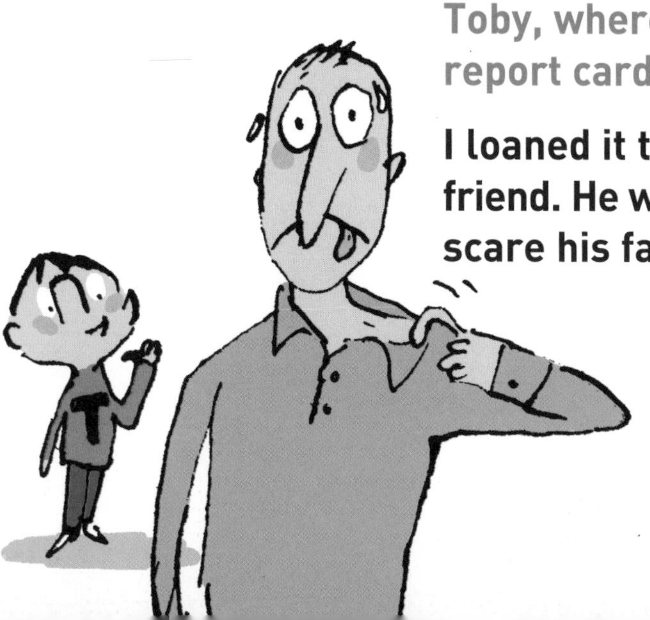

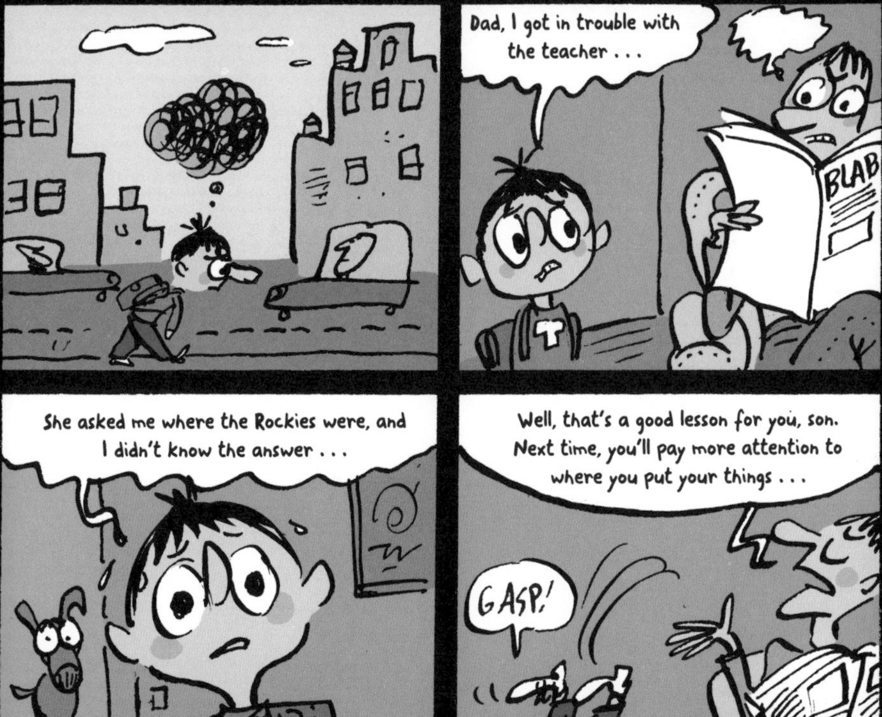
Dad, I got in trouble with the teacher . . .
BLAB
She asked me where the Rockies were, and I didn't know the answer . . .
Well, that's a good lesson for you, son. Next time, you'll pay more attention to where you put your things . . .
GASP!

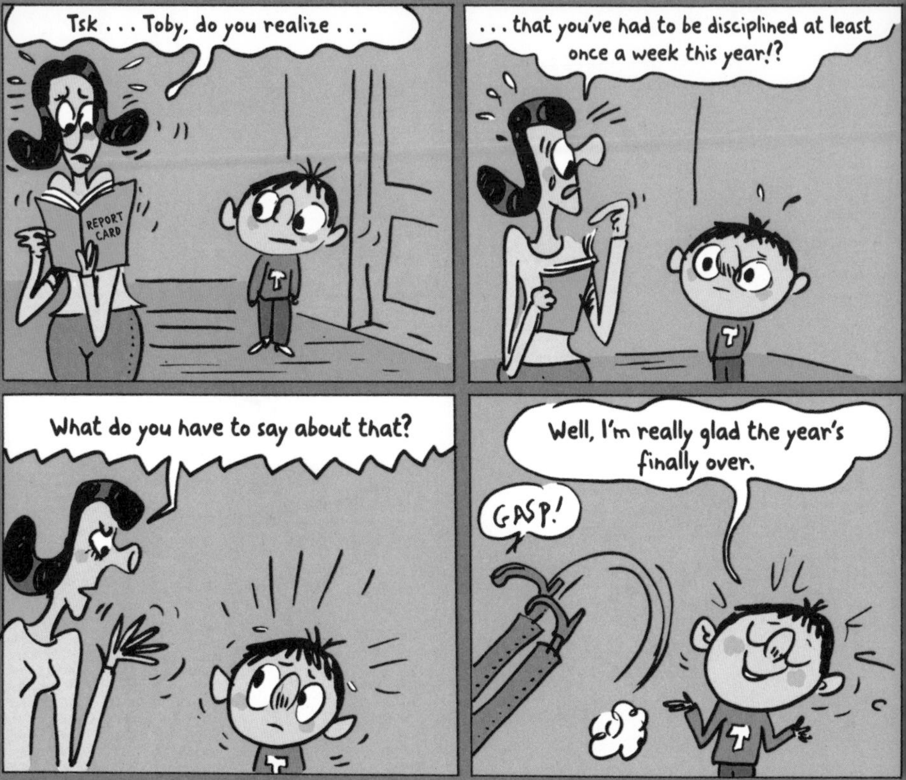
Tsk . . . Toby, do you realize . . .
REPORT CARD
. . . that you've had to be disciplined at least once a week this year!?
What do you have to say about that?
Well, I'm really glad the year's finally over.
GASP!

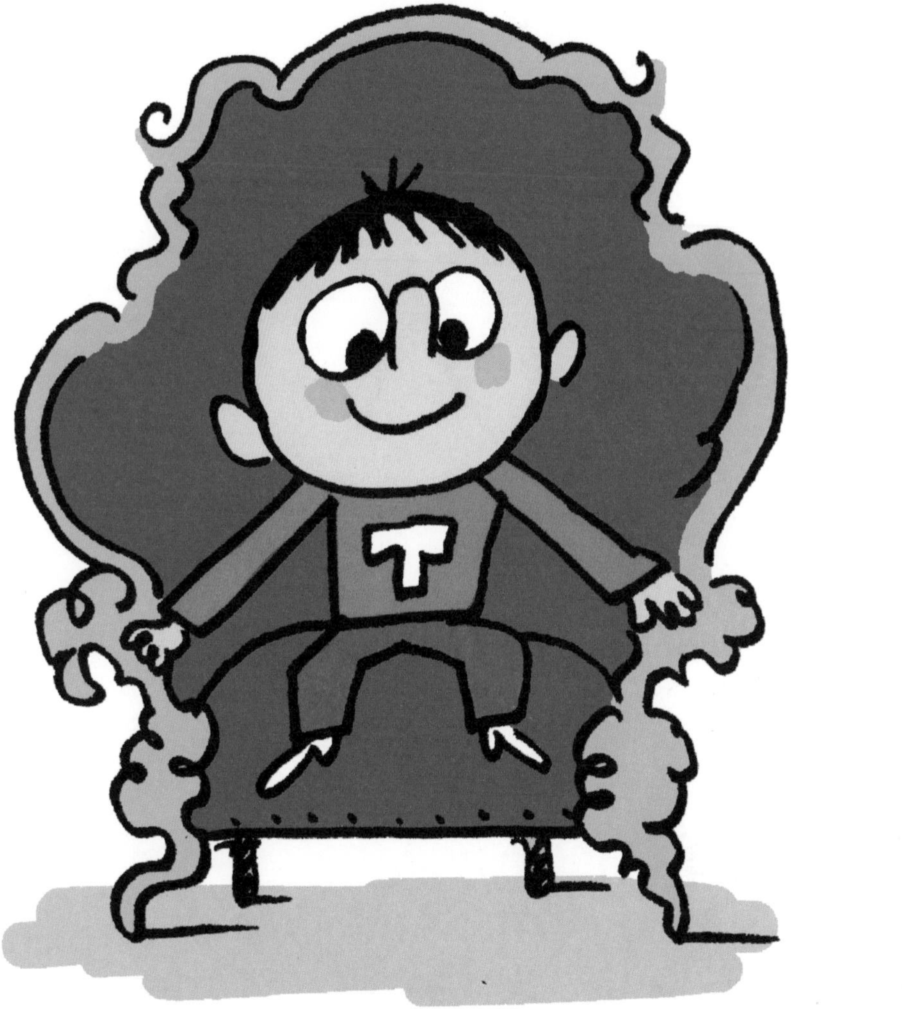
T

At the end of the day, a report card with low grades doesn't mean I'm not

AWESOME!

But Mom and Dad always
forgive me. And no matter
if I'm a good boy or I'm
a naughty boy, we still
have dinner together
as a family.

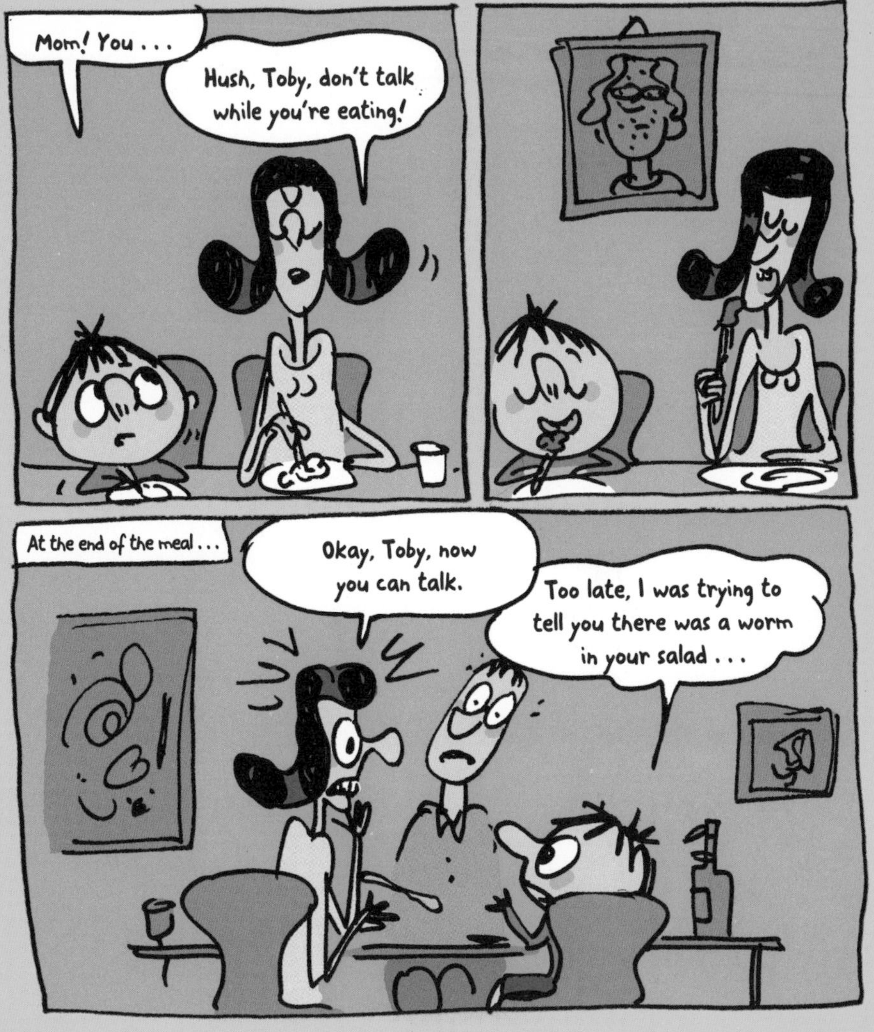
Mom! You . . .
Hush, Toby, don't talk while you're eating!
At the end of the meal . . .
Okay, Toby, now you can talk.
Too late, I was trying to tell you there was a worm in your salad . . .

And then it's time for bed. It's also the last time I get to mess with Dad before going to sleep!

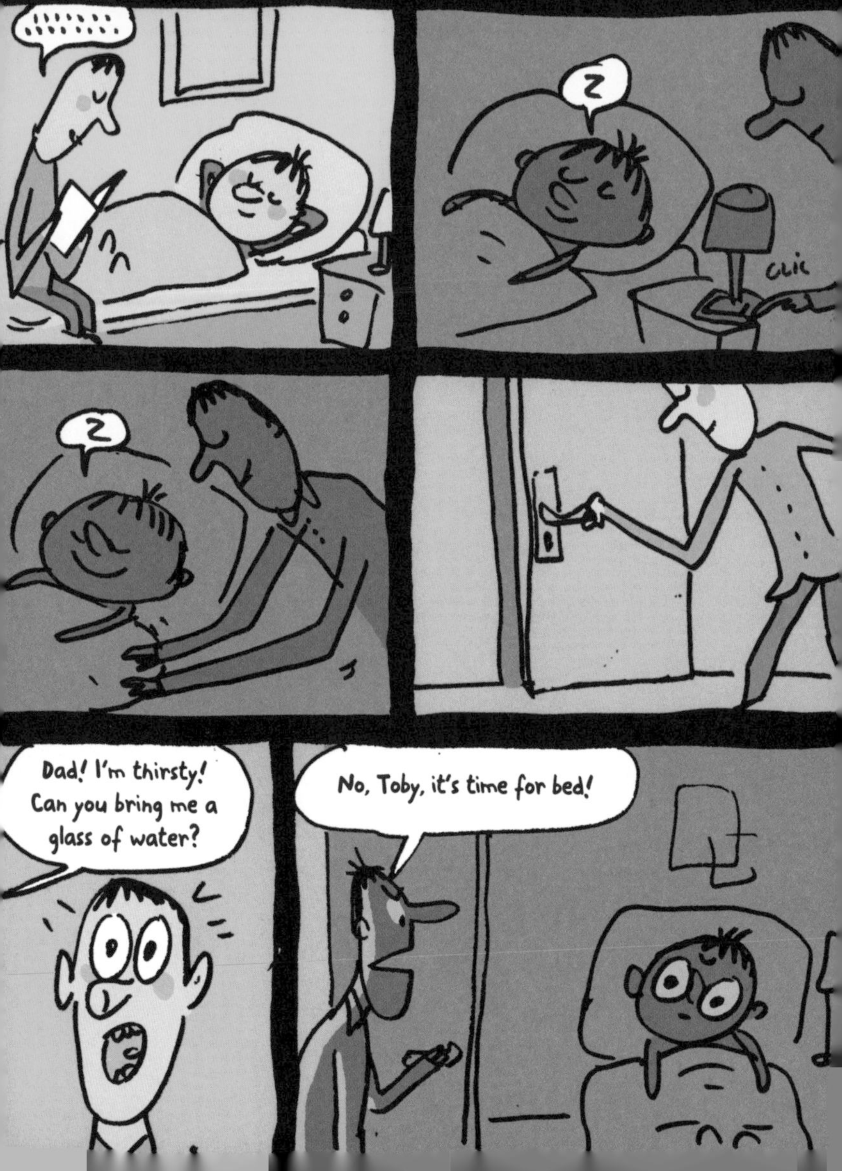
CLIC
Dad! I'm thirsty! Can you bring me a glass of water?
No, Toby, it's time for bed!

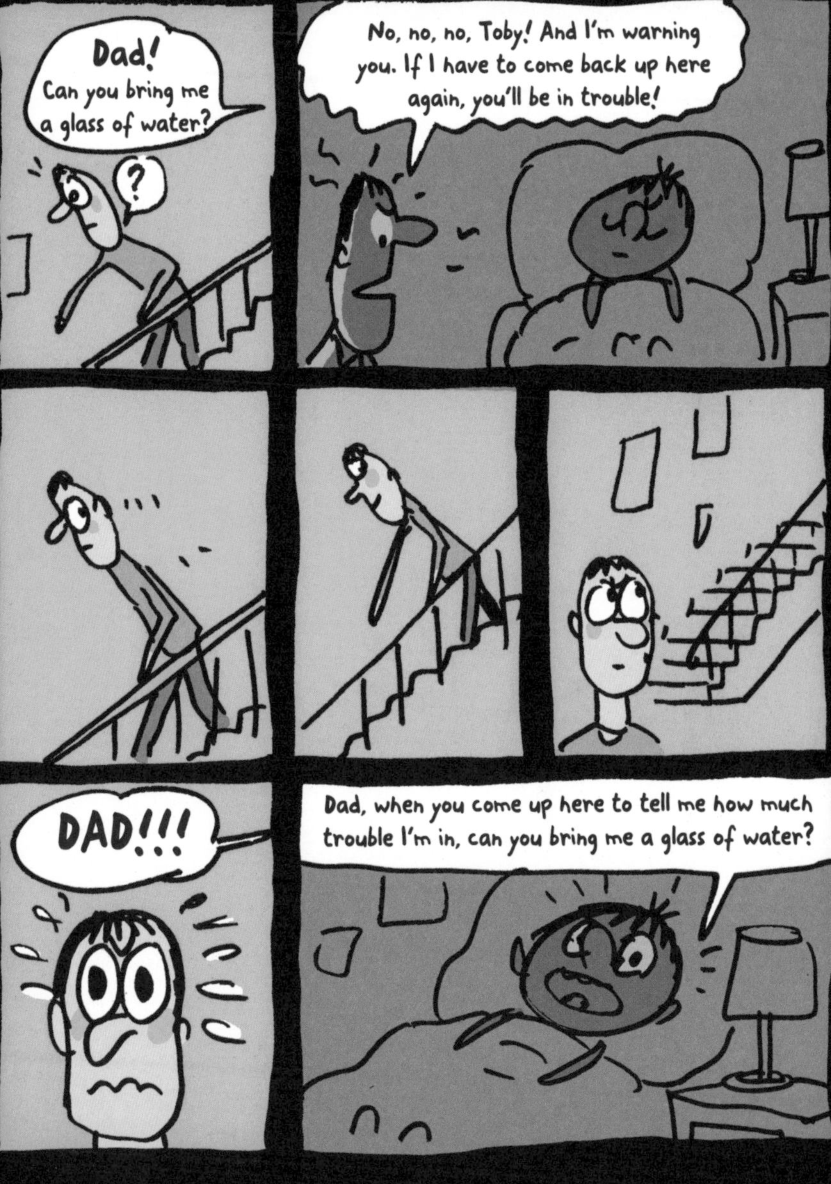
Dad!
Can you bring me a glass of water?
?
No, no, no, Toby! And I'm warning you. If I have to come back up here again, you'll be in trouble!
DAD!!!
Dad, when you come up here to tell me how much trouble I'm in, can you bring me a glass of water?

WELL, THAT'S MY LIFE!

Just a little part of it, anyway.

I do **LOTS** of other things that I don't have time to get into. Like **ALLIGATOR WRESTLING**, **SKYDIVING**, **WINNING OLYMPIC MEDALS**, **STOPPING BANK ROBBERS**. But you don't want to hear about any of that boring stuff!

Time to dream again!

HELLO!

AHHHH. Pure bliss.

Franck Girard is an author and publisher. After publishing children's books in major French houses such as Nathan, Bayard, and Milan for years, he created his own company, Tourbillon, and more recently its U.S. imprint, Twirl. A fan of comic books, Franck, who has been writing Toby's joke books for fifteen years, has brought great joy to the masses of French children.

Serge Bloch is a Society of Illustrators Gold Medal winner and recipient of France's Baobab Award. He has written and illustrated numerous books for children and young adults. He lives in Paris, France, and New York City.